Massacre at Red Rock

Liberty Jones is tired of war – he fought hard in the Civil War, saw great suffering and endured much himself. Now all he wants is to be left in peace, but trouble has a way of finding him. He rides into the town of Red Rock to escape a marauding tribe of Indians, but any hopes of safety he may have held are soon dispelled. For the town is under military command and facing a gathering of great Indian tribes who are determined to drive the people from the town and reclaim their land.

Liberty, along with a ragtag band of townspeople, must face impossible odds; soon blood will run deep in the streets of Red Rock.

Massacre at Red Rock

Jack Martin

A Black Horse Western

ROBERT HALE

© Jack Martin 2017
First published in Great Britain 2017

ISBN 978-0-7198-2222-3

The Crowood Press
The Stable Block
Crowood Lane
Ramsbury
Marlborough
Wiltshire SN8 2HR

www.bhwesterns.com

Robert Hale is an imprint
of The Crowood Press

Typeset by
Derek Doyle & Associates, Shaw Heath
Printed and bound in Great Britain by
CPI Group (UK) Ltd, Croydon, CR0 4YY

AUTHOR'S NOTE

The American Indian Wars were a complex and often brutal series of confrontations fought with great courage and ingenuity shown by both sides. In the writing of this novel, I have eschewed the modern ideology and avoided words or phrases like Native Americans. I have struggled with the modern concept of political correctness and then decided that it is not relevant to the story.

I have stuck to the terminology used during the period in which the story is set. Likewise some of the characters show attributes that today we would call, racist. But that was the time and place and it is a writer's duty to reflect as much reality as possible in any fiction for the deceit to work. However, artistic licence has been used with location and particularly the gathering together of the great tribes in the interest of telling a story.

Jack Martin

PROLOGUE

The Civil War had ended, the country was being rebuilt, the railroads extended. Men whose names would go down in history – Goodnight, Chisholm, Macahan – were driving thousands upon thousands of longhorn cattle across treacherous trails. Gold was being discovered across the West, and scores of whites ran rampant over grounds that had been promised to the Indians by the Great White Father; the vast plains once the preserve of the Indians and buffalo now rumbled to the sound of the iron horse.

Towns sprang up in the wilderness and grew at tremendous rates as the reconstruction started and slowly wealth began to return to a country ravaged by war. With this great expansion the American government once again moved the Indian tribes and once more the native peoples learned that the white father spoke with a forked tongue.

More and more whites came into the West and the Indians feared that their way of life would soon be gone, like so much sand in the wind.

Some fought back.

The town of Red Rock was less than six months old when the army moved in to protect the new settlers from the marauding Indians. It wasn't much of a town, occupying only three acres of ground. Plans were that it would grow but for now it consisted of a hotel, a saloon, a jailhouse, a livery stable and several unfinished buildings. The Indian attacks on the town had been ferocious and frequent. Army intelligence learned that a large band of Indians was gathering in the hills above Red Rock.

The government wanted the town to be here; it would serve as a feeder between Indian Territory and the railroads. So after the first Indian attacks the army had arrived with orders to protect the town at all costs, and lumber that had been intended for new commercial buildings was commandeered and used to construct a massive stockade wall around the town. From a distance the town looked like a large fort.

The War Between the States had been over but a short time and now the decades-old Indian wars were going to intensify in brutal and terrible ways.

CHAPTER ONE

'Liberty Jones,' Liberty said by way of introduction.

He climbed down from his horse, slid his rifle into its boot and smiled at the captain. He watched the troopers close the stockade gates, ran a hand over his sweaty brow and spat a globule of tobacco juice on to the ground.

'Never thought I'd be glad to see a Blue Belly,' he said.

'Keep a civil tongue in your mouth, Reb,' Captain Nathan Roberts snarled.

'Relax.' Liberty smiled. 'The war's over. We're all Americans now, leastways that's what they say.'

'The war may be over,' the captain said, prodding Liberty in the chest with a long fleshy finger, 'but the grass has barely grown over the battlefields. Don't much pay to be making jokes in a Southern accent.'

Liberty felt a wave of anger in his stomach but he controlled it. He was a little over thirty years old and had served valiantly in the War Between the States. He had seen action and bloodshed on the fields of conflict and much more besides.

'Can't help my accent,' he said. He didn't need this from this pompous cavalry captain, who didn't look so much battle-scarred as fat and weary.

'That may be so,' the captain said, 'but you can sure watch what you say. War or no war, Blue Belly is considered an insult.'

'We've another war to occupy us in any case,' Liberty said. He cast a look back towards the hastily constructed town gates. 'Something's sure riled up those Indians.'

'All it takes is the sight of white skin to rile them devils,' the captain said. He gestured for two of his men to take Liberty's horse to the livery stable. Horses were of vital importance in the current situation: far more valuable than a loud-mouthed ex-Confederate soldier. 'Consider yourself under my command.'

Liberty was about to protest but decided against it. He had just ridden past a massive Indian force and had barely made the town of Red Rock alive. It had been more luck than anything else that had kept him ahead of the pursuing Indians. For the moment he had nowhere else to go.

'How many men have you got?' Liberty asked. The captain took a slim cigar from his tunic and struck a match on his boot heel.

'There are just over two hundred souls in this town.'

'Does that include the women?' Liberty asked, pointing at a group of women who had congregated outside a large white tent. They seemed to be queuing for the food rations that were being handed out by a portly man in uniform. He was ladling dollops of a thick-looking stew into large wooden bowls.

'It does,' the captain said. 'There are two hundred-odd people here, including yourself. Sixty of us are women and children. The rest are able-bodied men.'

'How many soldiers amongst that lot?'

'The regiment consists of over ninety enlisted men.'

'Then God help us!' Liberty said. He had just seen an Indian war party that must have numbered at least a thousand braves. All in all the Indians seemed much better organized.

'We're severely outnumbered,' Liberty went on. 'When they attack it'll be in force. We won't be able to hold them for long.'

The captain smiled as if to dismiss the other man's warnings.

'Look around you,' he said. 'We can hold the savages off for ever if need be.'

True, the town had been turned into a fortress. The army had constructed a large wooden fence around the young town, and had built several sentry posts which were manned by armed men. Effectively they had constructed a fort around the new settlement. It offered some protection against the Indians but would not hold up indefinitely against onslaught after onslaught.

'You intend to fight, then?'

'We do,' the captain said. 'Reinforcements will be here in less than a week.'

'Could be too long,' Liberty told him. 'Far better to evacuate everyone and fight the Indians on the run. If they drive us away they may be satisfied with that and let us go in peace.'

'And what of the town?'

Liberty took a look around him.

Town? A hotel, a saloon, several nondescript wooden buildings, a jailhouse and a stack of unused lumber. Certainly it didn't look like anything worth dying for.

'It isn't much of a town,' he opined.

'Nevertheless the war office wants this town to grow. It will be of vital importance when the railroad starts towards Arizona.'

'Don't think the Indians want the town to grow.'

11

Liberty spat on to the dusty ground. 'That's why you're at odds.'

'The Indians will move on,' the captain said. 'Or they'll be moved by force. Congress demands it and I'm carrying out my orders.'

'It's Indian land,' Liberty said. 'They'll fight to the last man to protect it.'

The captain ignored him; it was patently obvious that the man saw the Indians as nothing more than mindless savages, offering no real threat to the trained military machine.

'Get yourself something to eat, Reb,' he said, brushing dust from his tunic. 'You'll be expected to fight with the rest of the men.'

'Naturally.' Liberty replied. He wandered over to the chuck wagon. For a moment he had considered pointing out that the word 'Reb' was as much of an insult as 'Blue Belly' but figured it wouldn't be worth wasting his breath.

He got himself a bowl of the stew and a piece of bread that had the texture of a small rock. Stew, vegetables and bread were the only items on the menu, but at that moment they were enough and his stomach rumbled in anticipation of the frugal meal. It had been days since he'd eaten anything other than wild berries and stale jerky. He took the meal over to a table that had been set up outside the saloon.

While Liberty chewed the tough beef and under-cooked vegetables he kept his eyes busy watching events up and down the one and only street.

The group of women he'd seen queuing for food were eating at a table outside the chuck wagon, but they seemed too involved in their conversation to pay him much heed. A number of men both in and out of uniform walked up and down the street. A few other people, mostly men, milled around with seemingly nothing to do, and a couple of children ran up the street, a flea-bitten dog barking at their heels. The sentry posts, known as pigeon roosts were manned, each contained a Blue Belly armed with a rifle. Over in the far corner a bunch of men, all civilians, were being put through their paces by a sergeant.

The small town was completely enclosed within the stockade walls, which gave Liberty a feeling of confinement. It wasn't a feeling he was particularly fond of. He had spent months in a prisoner-of-war camp towards the end of the recent conflict and now, barely a blink of an eye since hostilities had ended, he was once again facing imprisonment of a sort.

He looked across the street and saw the army commander chatting with the captain and another portly man who wore a sergeant's stripes. They seemed to be assessing the current situation and, although Liberty couldn't hear what was being said, it was obvious from their troubled expressions that things were not going as well as they'd like.

The town of Red Rock was under siege.

CHAPTER TWO

'Mind if I join you, old boy?' the man asked in a cultured English accent.

Liberty peered up from his food and looked into the face of a most extraordinary-looking man. He man was wearing the cleanest, sharpest clothes Liberty had ever seen: a gaudily checked suit in sandy colours, a dazzling white shirt with a stiff starched collar, and a neatly tied necktie. He had long blond hair that poked out from under the brim of his bowler hat. A well-trimmed salt-and-pepper moustache gave him an air of maturity that made it difficult to put an age to him. There were deeply etched lines around the Englishman's eyes that suggested he had seen a fair bit of life, but there was also a certain youthfulness about him.

'Thank you,' the man said without waiting for an invitation. He sat down, removed his hat, placed it on the table beside him and spooned a mouthful of the stew into his mouth. He pulled a face.

'Dreadful. Quite simply dreadful.'

'I've had worse,' Liberty said, using a piece of stale bread to mop the last of his own stew.

'I'm Lord Simon Sinclair,' the Englishman said, holding out a hand. 'I come from Bath, in England. Most pleased to meet you.'

Liberty stared at the Englishman's hand but didn't take the offer.

'Liberty,' he said. 'Plain old Liberty.'

'Liberty,' Sinclair repeated. 'Strange name. Why, that's the strangest name I ever did hear.' He laughed and spooned in another mouthful of the thick stew.

'My pa named me,' Liberty said. 'I guess he held deep convictions.'

'Makes sense, I suppose,' the Englishman said. 'In an American sort of way.'

'Sure.' Liberty spoke through a mouthful of stew.

'Well, you won't find much in the way of liberty here,' Sinclair said. He stirred the stew around the bowl with a wooden spoon. 'If I'd had any idea I'd end up like this – little more than a prisoner in this town – I'd never have come West.'

'Why did you?'

The Englishman looked at Liberty, then smiled.

'Gold and sin,' he replied. 'Gold and sin, old boy.'

'You don't look like a miner.'

'Perceptive of you,' Sinclair said. He forced an undercooked chunk of potato into his mouth. He chewed it rapidly and then swallowed. 'I'm a gambler. A card player and, if I say so myself, a damn good one.'

Liberty nodded. He knew the type of man: bone idle, always chasing easy riches and avoiding any kind of real work.

'I was on the stage to Tucson,' Sinclair continued. 'The town is booming but we were set upon by the red savages and had no option but to come into this sorry excuse for a town. I should have known it was a bad idea when I saw the army constructing the walls.'

'How long you been here?' Liberty asked.

'A little over a week. Seems longer.' The Englishman sighed. 'Much longer.'

'I guess this is the safest place at the moment,' Liberty said. He used more bread to mop the last of his stew and chewed but it crumbled in his mouth. He swallowed and even though his stomach still felt empty he decided that he had benefited from the meal. He suddenly felt the urge for a smoke.

'I'd rather take my chances and head on for

17

Tucson myself,' Sinclair said. 'I can look after myself but the army insist I stay put. They say it's for my own protection, but I've always looked after myself.'

'Fought many Indians, then?'

'No,' Sinclair conceded. 'But I dare say it shouldn't prove too difficult for a superior man such as myself. I've seen action, old boy, and I shouldn't think Indians are harder to kill than any other kind of man.'

'You killed many men?' Liberty asked.

'Only when I've had to,' Sinclair replied.

Liberty nodded. He was about to get up and leave the annoying English lord to his food and inane chatter when the military bugle sounded, screaming out its alarm. Gunfire erupted from the pigeon roosts and as Liberty looked up he saw one of the sentries struck by an arrow. The man threw his arms up in the air and then fell forward, rolling over the protective barrier and crashing to the hard ground some thirty feet below.

'Once again we're under attack,' Sinclair said calmly and continued eating his stew. He chewed the lumps of meat seemingly unconcerned about the chaos that was going on around him.

Liberty looked at the man, said nothing.

'Confounded Indians don't seem to have any sense of timing,' Sinclair complained. 'That's the trouble with savages – no idea of the social niceties.'

Liberty looked at the Englishman for a moment, then shrugged his shoulders. He had come across some odd sorts over the years but he didn't think he had seen a stranger man than this English lord. He rose to his feet, placed a hand on one of his Colts and cleared leather.

'Can you hit anything with those things?' The voice had come from behind Liberty. He spun round and saw the sergeant whom he had seen training the civilians earlier, a burly man with a barrel chest and stern features.

'I generally hit what I aim for,' Liberty said.

'Then get to the walls,' the sergeant said. 'Fire through the slits.'

'Sure.' Liberty nodded. He noticed that the Englishman was still eating his meal as if oblivious of all that was going on around him.

Liberty went to a free slit in the wall, positioning himself between two soldiers. He peered through the makeshift opening and could see a party of perhaps fifty Indians circling the town. There were Apaches, Sioux and Navajos among them; tribes that were usually mortal enemies had joined forces.

He caught an Indian in his sights and fired, watching grimly as his bullet took the brave square in the face. Blood and gore sprayed into the air as the Indian fell backwards from his terrified horse.

Liberty took no pleasure in killing Indians and could see that it was the white man's encroachment on their lands that had turned them hostile. He had lived with Indians and knew that they were mostly peaceable until threatened.

'You got one of the redskins!' the soldier to Liberty's left exclaimed. 'Good shoo—' His words were cut short as a perfectly aimed arrow came through the slit in the wall and buried itself dead centre in his forehead. His legs buckled beneath him and he fell to the ground, the arrow still buried in his head. His legs and arms kicked with involuntary muscle spasms even though he was already dead.

'And one of them's got you,' Liberty observed grimly. He fired again. Sinclair stepped over the fallen soldier and smiled at Liberty.

'Mind if I join you?' he asked, as if he were requesting an invitation to some sort of social gathering. 'This one seems to be sleeping this one out.'

'It ain't my party,' Liberty said, smiling slightly at the Englishman's grim humour. Again he looked the man up and down. 'You armed?'

'Indeed.' Sinclair pulled a strange-looking gun from his jacket. It was roughly the size of a standard Colt but Liberty had never seen a gun quite like it. There were intricate patterns etched into its barrel; they continued along the weapon and on to the ivory butt. The trigger seemed to be made of a different metal from the rest of the gun and was a dull black in colour. It was mighty pretty but in the current situation it wasn't ornamental value that mattered.

'I hope you can shoot it,' Liberty said. He fired several shots through the slit in the walls. He hugged the wall as a storm of arrows fell out of the sky and landed all around them. He sighted an Indian and fired again, taking him in the stomach and lifting him off his horse.

The Englishman fired with the skill of a true marksman through the slit that the soldier had forsaken. He let off three shots in quick succession and with each one he saw an Indian drop.

'Does that answer your question?' Sinclair asked. He took aim and fired again.

'Damn!' Liberty said and fired another shot of his own.

The bugle sounded and Liberty watched as the Indians rode away in retreat. There looked to be more leaving for the safety of their camp than had been left behind, dead or wounded. All in all it was not a good result. Liberty slid his Colt into its holster and looked at the Englishman with a curious eye.

'You've got hidden depths,' he said.

'Why, thank you,' Sinclair said. 'Can I buy you a

drink?' He pointed to the saloon.

Liberty looked around them. There were several dead soldiers on the ground, all with arrows embedded in them. There was a fire blazing away in one of the sentry posts; its being so high up meant that no one had any option but to let it burn. He estimated that they had lost maybe half a dozen men, all of them soldiers.

'Why not?' he replied.

They had just started across the street when Captain Roberts spied them. After barking a few commands to several men he came over to them.

'Where do you think you're going?' he asked.

'For a drink,' Sinclair said with a lopsided grin. 'Fighting the natives can be thirsty business.'

'I think not,' the captain said. 'Fall in with the rest of the men. There's work to be done.'

'We'll fight,' Liberty said, not realizing that he had suddenly elected himself as spokesman for them both. 'But we ain't gonna be available to your every whim.'

'Insubordinate!' the captain said furiously. 'I'll have you put in the stocks for this.'

'Sure,' Liberty said. 'But everyone looks kinda busy just now, so we'll wait over in the saloon.'

'Yes,' Sinclair said. 'When you've readied the shackles be a decent chap and bring them over.'

With that he and Liberty walked across the street

to the saloon, both of them aware that the fat captain was breathing like a frustrated bull behind them.

'I think we've upset him,' Sinclair said.

Liberty smiled. 'You don't say,' he replied.

The saloon was the only place in the makeshift town that seemed to be open for business as usual. Neither Liberty nor Sinclair gave this circumstance much thought, but pushed the batwings wide and went inside.

'That was some mighty fine shooting.' Liberty took a slug of whiskey. They had taken the bottle from a rat-faced man behind the counter and seated themselves in a corner booth with a view of the batwings. They could clearly hear the bustle of activity going on outside the saloon.

'One needs to be able to defend oneself when travelling in such an hostile land,' Sinclair said. He took a mouthful of the whiskey, then immediately topped his glass up.

'You can sure enough do that,' Liberty said. 'What kind of gun is that?'

'This,' Sinclair pulled the pistol from the shoulder holster he wore beneath his jacket, 'is a Hopkins and Allen gold-plated revolver. Quite unique in its design. I had it made to my specifications in Manchester, England.'

'Don't go much for embellishments myself,' Liberty said. 'But I guess it serves its purpose.'

'That's the problem with you Americans,' the Englishman said with a wry smile. He sipped at his own drink. 'So vulgar. No sense of style.'

'Looks like trouble,' Liberty said, nodding towards the batwings.

Captain Roberts accompanied by two heavily armed troopers crossed the floor of saloon and stood over their table. The fat man glared down at the two men for a moment, then a smile crossed his lips.

'Arrest these men,' he ordered the troopers.

Sinclair still had his gun in his hand and for a moment it looked as if he was going to challenge the soldiers, but then he placed it back into the shoulder holster beneath his jacket. He downed his whiskey and poured another from the bottle, which he offered to Liberty.

'No.' Liberty shook his head and pushed his chair back from the table.

Sinclair shrugged and proceeded to down the whiskey himself.

'I don't believe I'll be arrested today,' Liberty said. He let his arms hang at his sides, poised to make a play for his gun at the first movement from any of the Blue Belly.

'Gentlemen,' Sinclair stood and positioned

himself between Liberty and the captain, 'might I ask what we are being arrested for?'

'For refusing to obey orders,' the captain told him.

'But we're not military, old boy,' Sinclair pointed out. 'You have no authority over us.'

The captain gave the Englishman a puzzled look.

'This is a siege situation,' he said. 'I have the authority to place this town under martial law and until I say otherwise every able-bodied man in this town will consider himself to be under military command. That includes you and the Reb.'

'Well, why didn't you say?' Sinclair smiled. 'Why, we'd be delighted to accompany you to your jail-house.'

'What?' Liberty said.

Sinclair looked at Liberty, then shrugged his shoulders. 'Well, come on. Let's not keep the good captain waiting. He must be a very busy man.'

Liberty frowned; then, despite his annoyance, he allowed himself to relax.

'Arrest these men,' the captain repeated.

'No need to be unpleasant,' Sinclair said. 'As I've said, we'll gladly accompany you to the jailhouse.'

Liberty looked first at the soldiers and then at the Englishman. He was not at all sure what was happening here. Everything had taken on a surreal edge and he felt removed from events, like a spectator of his own life.

'Come on, then.' Sinclair got to his feet and slapped Liberty upon the shoulder. 'Let's not keep these men waiting. They've got a lot to do.'

Liberty exchanged puzzled glances with the troopers, then calmly followed them out of the saloon and across the street to the jailhouse. It was all very civilized and made being arrested less of an indignity than was usual.

CHAPTER THREE

'I don't believe what just happened,' Liberty said. He stared at the bars of the cell. 'Did I just relinquish my weapons and allow myself to be placed here without so much as a struggle?'

'You did, old boy,' Sinclair agreed. He was seated upon an upturned bucket, legs crossed one over the other, in the next cell; he appeared to be examining his fingernails for dirt. There was a third cell but its occupant, a scrawny old man, was seemingly in a deep sleep and oblivious to their presence.

'Remind me never to listen to you again, English,' Liberty said. He sat himself down on the hard bunk that took up most of his own cell.

He kicked his own bucket clattering into the bars.

The old-timer stirred but continued snoring.

'You would have got into a fight with that insufferable captain,' Sinclair said, not unreasonably.

'Likely I would have,' Liberty agreed. 'I'd like nothing better than to pound some sense into that man.'

'Well, I may have just saved you from a firing squad.' Sinclair smiled.

'Might have had more chance with a firing squad,' Liberty said.

'I really don't see that,' Sinclair replied. He worried something out from under one of his fingernails and flicked it across the cell. 'Dirt and dust everywhere you look.'

'This town is surrounded by hostile Indians,' Liberty pointed out. 'Sooner or later they're going to break through the defences and storm this town. We'll be sitting ducks locked in here.'

'Oh, we'll be out long before that happens,' Sinclair said. He seemed to have finished with his nails, now he stood up and stretched, working a kink out of his back. 'I think I'll get some sleep before they release us.' He lay back on the bunk and pulled his bowler down over his eyes.

'You seem sure they'll let us out.' Liberty took the makings from his shirt pocket and rolled a quirly. He struck a sulphur match on the hard floor and soon had himself a smoke going.

'The captain's not holding up to the stresses and strains of the frontier life,' Sinclair said. As he was speaking from underneath the bowler hat his words were slightly muffled. 'Once the commander learns we're in here he'll order our release. What good can two able-bodied men do, locked away, when the army need all hands to fight what seems to be the entire Indian population of America?' He sat up, pushed his hat back on his head and smiled at Liberty. 'We'll be out of here before nightfall.'

'You seem pretty sure of that.'

'I'd wager my life, old boy.'

It made a certain kind of sense, but Liberty had just come away from four years in the military, the final months spent in a Union prison camp, and he knew how illogical the military mind could be. As far as he was concerned allowing himself to get locked up like this was the height of folly and he still didn't understand just what had happened. He had been dragged along in the moment and now it all seemed unreal to him, as if it hadn't taken place at all. It almost felt like this was happening to someone else, that at any moment he'd wake from a dream.

'Shut the hell up!' The words, coming from the old-timer's cell, were followed by an even more colourful string of expletives. Liberty and the Englishman looked at each other.

The old man was awake.

'How's a fella supposed to sleep?' the old man

asked. 'Nothing else to do in this stinking hole than sleep. Sooner you two quit jawing the better I'm gonna like it.'

'Dreadfully sorry, old man,' Sinclair said.

'The floor would be more comfortable than this flea-ridden bed,' the old man groused. He sat on the edge of his bunk and scratched his head. He shifted his position, farted, then followed up with a deep-throated belch. Bleary eyed, he looked at the newcomers and then shook his head.

'I thought I'd have this place all to myself,' the old man grumbled, rubbing his face. He seemed to be having trouble coming round, as if he had been sleeping off a heavy drinking session.

'What you doing in there, old-timer?' Liberty asked.

'I was sleeping,' the old man said, 'until you two turned up and started raising a ruckus.'

'What my companion means,' Sinclair explained as if to a child, 'is that, assuming you don't choose to sleep in a jailhouse cell and you've not got a penchant for hard floors and the confinement of incarceration, then what are you doing here? Of what indiscretion are you guilty?'

The old-timer stared in puzzlement at the Englishman, and then at Liberty for an interpretation of the florid language, but all he got from Liberty was a shrug of the shoulders and a puzzled frown. The look seemed to say, Don't ask me.

'What did you do, old boy?' Sinclair prompted with a sigh.

The old man smiled as the penny dropped.

'I've been put in here for my own safety,' he said.

'Elucidate, old man,' Sinclair said.

Again the old man gave a puzzled glance at Liberty. The Englishman was clearly an alien species to him.

'I think he means tell it all,' Liberty said. He drew on the last of his smoke and flicked the stub into the corner of his cell. The old man nodded.

'They don't like me wandering around out in the wilds with the Indians on the warpath. An army scouting party found me a few miles away a little over ten days ago and insisted on rescuing me. I didn't need no rescuing but they won't listen. They brought me here and when I escaped they brought me back again. When I escaped a second time they threw me in here. Now they won't release me because they know I'll skip town again. I'm stuck here until this all ends.'

'How long you been locked up?' Liberty asked.

'Three or four days this time,' the old man answered glumly. 'Think so, anyway. The days stretch into one another in here.'

'Why would you want to leave?' Sinclair asked. 'With the Indians on the warpath one would

31

presume it would be safer to remain with the army.'

'It's the army that riled the Indians in the first place,' the old man said. 'The Indians have no reason to wish me harm.'

'That's as maybe,' Sinclair said. 'Though I wouldn't want to try my chances out there. You want to lose your scalp, old man?'

'It's my scalp,' the old man retorted.

'Indeed it is,' Sinclair agreed. 'Still, I see no reason for taking needless risks.'

Liberty looked through the bars of his cell at the old man. He stared deeply into his face. He too was interested in the reasons for the old man's death wish. There was no way he'd be able to survive out in the open with so many warring Indians about. It must be something important to make him want to try.

Something worth risking his life for.

'I have my reasons,' the old man said. He refused to be drawn further on the matter.

CHAPTER FOUR

Chayton walked amongst his people.

They were all his people now: Apache, Sioux, Comanche, Kiowa, both Northern and Southern Cheyenne, Ute, Pawnee, Arapaho and even a scattering of Modoc warriors from beyond the Rogue River. Tribes that were more often than not mortal foes had united to fight the common enemy: the whites. They had all answered the call to the gathering and sent braves to take part in this concerted effort to drive the white man from the land; to drive the invader away once and for all. The Indian force now numbered over five thousand braves and more would be arriving imminently. Word had arrived only this morning that over five hundred braves from the Shoshoni were coming. Their messenger said they were but hours away.

It was an uneasy alliance but one that all considered necessary in order to defeat the white enemy. Tribes that had previously been bitter foes had come together as one. Past troubles, if not forgotten, were at least cast aside until the whites should be driven from these lands. Once this was all over, once the final drop of white blood had been spilled, the tribes would no doubt once again take to warring amongst themselves, but that was the way of the people; the stakes were greater in the war with the whites. When they fought amongst themselves they were fighting for control of land, honour, a woman even, but against the white invader the Indians were fighting for their very existence.

The gathering of the great tribes had come together in answer to a vision that had come to Chayton a little over two summers gone. Within the vision he saw the landscape littered with the dead bodies of the whites, saw the land growing again and claiming the dead bodies; he saw the return of the great buffalo hordes, he saw also an end to the virulent sickness that ravaged his people in greater numbers than any war ever had. The vision told Chayton that his people would find a new paradise in which all of the tribes could prosper, away from the pestilence the whites called progress. He had at first told his own people of his vision and had then

34

acted out the vision in a bizarre dance that he called 'The Gathering'.

Wandering braves had witnessed the dance, understood its message and then taken that dance to their own tribes. The dance and the vision it contained had spread from tribe to tribe, taking on a life of its own. The dance told of a great victory and the turning of the tide, but only if the people – all the people – came together for The Gathering.

This was the wish of the Great Spirit.

The dance could be understood by all of the people; it transcended language, went beyond tribal barriers, speaking in movement and gesture. The dance ended with the return of the Great Spirit, heralding a thousand summers of peace and bounty for the indigenous people of the land that the whites now called America.

Chayton was cautious and would not take needless risks. He remembered the first time he had ridden into battle. That was over thirty summers ago but there were many parallels between then and now.

Then he had ridden with a band made up of mixed tribes. Then his enemies had been the whites.

Then he had carried his lance.

Then he had been a young brave, eager for his first kill.

Now, though, he was an experienced and respected chief with countless kills to his name. Many scalps adorned his lance and there were just as many scars upon his flesh.

He held his shoulders back and pushed his chest forward as he made his way to the fire at the centre of the camp. It was there that he would find the chiefs of all the tribes gathered. Although he had been given overall command he knew that he must discuss any move with the others. They were all wise men and commanded the respect and loyalty of their respective peoples, and as such it was foolish to discount any of them. Their wisdom had to be heard. They would all get his respect.

'I want to send out a war party,' he said as he reached the ten men seated around the blazing fire. 'To intercept the coming white man's reinforcements. To wipe them out if possible.'

'How many braves?' The question came from White Bird, the Sioux chief from the Great Plains.

'Two hundred men,' Chayton said.

'A large number,' White Bird noted.

Chayton nodded. 'But essential for success. The army reinforcements will be heavily armed and well trained. I have looked at our situation and I feel we can take the town within the week. Once we have burned it to the ground the white devils will have nothing to fight for. We will have won, but if the fresh soldiers get here before the town falls it could tip the balance. We are many but the soldiers have the better guns. It is these guns, not the skill and bravery of the warriors, that will win the battle. This the white men understand.'

'How do we know the white men have more soldiers coming?' White Bird asked. Chayton nodded. It was a good question.

'A Sioux scout brought the news,' he said. 'There is a large party of men, all wearing the blue uniform of the Great White Father. They are still beyond the Heart Mountains, perhaps five or six days away. They number maybe five hundred but they have the medicine guns that spit death in all directions at once. I have seen these guns used while I was watching many of the great battles between the whites. One of these weapons can cut down a thousand men in the blink of an eye.'

'We are strong,' Running Elk, a Kiowa, said. 'We can repel any men who come. The Great Spirit is with us.'

'We *are* strong,' Chayton said. 'This is true, and we are many, but the white men are bad medicine. The longer this fight goes on the more chance the white men have of gaining the upper hand. The reinforcements will only be the first wave. More will come.' Chayton had been at several major battles with the whites, among them Adobe Walls and

37

Kildeer Mountain, and he knew they were a deadly force. He would not underestimate them.

'The white man's war has left them weak,' Running Elk said. 'They have no stomach for a fight.'

'The white men have the thirst for killing,' Chayton countered. 'They are a worthy enemy.'

He fell silent, looking into the flames, remembering times past and fearing an uncertain future to come. Lately his visions had shown a land he did not recognize, yet he knew it to be his own. It had been built upon, developed, the ground had been suffocated until where there once had been green now there was only sand. He kept these doubts to himself, for he had initiated The Gathering; it was his visions that had brought them all together.

Choolay, leader of the Eastern Apache people and a renowned warrior himself, looked deep into the flames of the small fire.

'True, the whites are weakened,' he said. 'But their numbers are escalating. They can not be trusted and we must do whatever we can to defeat them before it is too late.'

Murmurs of agreement passed from one man to another and Chayton gave a smile at their words. Choolay was a man of vision and his was a similar vision to the one he himself held.

'Where today are the Pequot?' Choolay continued. 'Where are the Narragansett, the Mohican and many other once powerful tribes? The white man came upon our land like a great pestilence and too many true people have vanished like the snow before the sun. I agree with Chayton. More of our people will be arriving soon and I feel we can spare a couple of hundred braves. More if necessary. We will not let ourselves be destroyed by the white men.'

'The Great Spirit demands that we fight and we shall fight,' White Bird said; his words carried steel. 'This gathering of the different tribes does indeed show us we are one people. We shall destroy the white man once and for all.'

'Blood shall run in the name of The Great Spirit,' Chayton concurred.

He understood the need to take full advantage of the current situation. The white men had been left weak after their war between themselves but this would not last for ever. Already they were gaining strength and confidence and were starting to move back into areas of the West that had been left deserted during their war. Soon they would start to thrive and be joined by ever greater numbers.

The plague of the white man was coming.

'We will support you,' White Bird said after a long silence. 'Your visions are true. We trust in them.'

'Thank you.' Chayton smiled at each of the men in turn. 'I will raise a war party immediately and send it out. It will meet the coming men many miles from here. Even if the white men are in greater numbers than our people we shall at least slow them down. Time is all we need to drive away these people who poison our land like a disease of the soil itself.'

'When that is done,' Running Elk said, 'when we have destroyed the town that the whites call Red Rock, and have nourished the tainted soil with their blood we shall move on. Wherever we find the white men we shall drive them away or kill them where they stand.'

'Good.' Chayton nodded. 'Then I shall select the men.' With that he walked away, leaving the wise men gathered around the fire.

Chayton felt that two hundred warriors would be sufficient. It would be just enough for them to stand a chance of overwhelming the whites before they could use their medicine guns. Sending any more would make it difficult to effect the surprise that afforded the best chance they had of winning against the soldiers and their formidable weapons. If they could capture even one of these guns and figure out how it worked they would be able to bring hell to the whites.

He sought out Chail, his most trusted brave, and

instructed him to move amongst the tribes at the great gathering and select those he felt best suited to the mission ahead.

CHAPTER FIVE

Liberty stood on his bunk and peered through the small window into the alleyway between the jail-house and the saloon. The sky was darkening and had turned a curious gunmetal grey. There was a storm coming and the taste of static hung heavy in the air.

'I don't like being cooped up in here,' he said. He jumped down and sat on the edge of his bunk. He looked first at the Englishman and then at the old-timer but neither man said anything. If there was a storm and the Indians took advantage of it, using it as cover to attack, then the last place he wanted to be was in here, unarmed, unable to defend himself.

'We'll be out of here soon enough,' Sinclair repeated.

'You seem darn sure, English.'

'I am.' Sinclair was steadfast in his resolve.

'You'll rot in here just like me,' the old man said. He started laughing, his mouth opening wide enough to reveal the three ragged teeth that remained in his gums, looking like weathered tombstones.

'Old man,' Sinclair said, 'if you don't stop that cackling I'll strangle you with my bare hands.'

The old man regarded both Liberty and the Englishman for a moment; then he shook his head.

'You don't scare me none,' he said.

'Easy to say when we can't get to you,' Sinclair said.

Liberty smiled and made to lunge at the bars of the old man's cell, but he sat down when the old man recoiled as if fearing the younger man would magically pass through the bars and appear in his cell. The old man spat.

'Strewth!' he said. 'You two don't know who you're messing with.'

'Just some old fool,' Sinclair said.

'Fool? Is Billy the Kid a fool?' The old man's voice took on a strength that belied his advanced years. 'You two ever heard of Billy the Kid?'

'Billy the Kid?' Sinclair jumped up, a look of awe upon his face, but then the look was quickly replaced by one of amusement. 'No. Never heard of him.'

'Son of a bitch!' the old man said, then lay down on his bunk. He pulled the thick blanket over himself and curled up in a foetal position.

'Is that you?' Liberty asked. 'You seem mighty long in the tooth to be calling yourself any kind of kid.'

'I used to be known as such,' the old man said, pride audible in his words. 'I used to be.'

Despite his mood Liberty smiled, then looked grimly towards the window. The coming storm worried him and he was feeling more confined than ever. Like a wild animal trapped in a snare, he was unable to relax and his nerves were on edge. He felt that at any moment now he'd go stark raving mad. He had lived with Indians and knew how they thought. The storm would provide adequate cover for men skilled in warfare, men able to blend in with the night and become almost invisible. They would become one with the night and enter the town like ghosts, unseen until they launched the first attack.

For a moment there was silence; then the jail-house door opened and a pretty young woman entered carrying a tray which held three bowls of the thick stew that seemed to be all anyone ever ate around here. Captain Roberts and a tall, cadaverously thin man wearing the insignia of commander followed her in. Behind these men walked two fresh-faced troopers.

Outside the sky grew darker still and the rumbling of distant thunder sounded louder as it approached the beleaguered town. Rain started to fall ever more fiercely until it sounded like an almighty deluge.

'I'm Commander Brown,' the commander said. 'I'm here to remedy this situation.'

The young woman handed a bowl of stew to each of the men in the cells through the gaps in the cell bars. She didn't make eye contact with any of them and blushed when the Englishman made a comment about her being a ray of light in the darkness. Lightning flashed outside, briefly illuminating the interior of the jailhouse. The girl's eyes seemed to glow and reflect the white light, causing her pupils to sparkle.

She was certainly a beauty, Liberty thought.

'What do you propose?' Sinclair asked. He took a mouthful of the thick stew and winced as he chewed the overcooked beef. If he ever escaped the jailhouse and then the dammed town the first thing he was going to do was get himself a real meal. A dish where the meat was soft and succulent and the vegetables had actually been cooked rather than simply shown boiling water.

'You two are of no use locked away in here,' the commander said. 'We need every man we can get to defend this town.'

'Then let us out,' Sinclair said and for the briefest of moments he made eye contact with the young woman. She again blushed and turned away, then pushed past the two troopers and went outside into the rain.

Brown smiled. 'It's not that simple,' he said.

'Why not?' Sinclair asked.

'Seems easy enough to me,' Liberty said. 'You unlock the door and we step out. Pretty simple really.'

A look passed between the captain and commander, then the captain saluted his superior, turned on his heel and left the jailhouse.

'I realize you men are not military,' Brown said. 'But if we are to survive onslaught after onslaught and protect the women and children we must have discipline. Until this is over you will have to obey orders just as the men in uniform obey orders. Consider yourselves temporary soldiers.'

Liberty nodded. 'Sounds fair enough to me,' he said. 'But your captain gets heavy handed. I'll do my bit in any fight but I won't take to being pushed around by that bag of wind.'

Lightning flashed again; this time it seemed like a number of powerful flashes that illuminated the inside of the jailhouse with the power of several suns. A huge thunderclap followed almost immediately, seeming to shake the very foundations of the jail-house.

For a moment it looked as if the commander was going to defend his captain, telling Liberty that he would follow his orders or stay locked away indefinitely, but then he nodded.

'We are all under strain,' he said. 'That includes the captain. I will speak to him on your behalf.'

'You do that,' Liberty said.

'Now do we have a deal?' the commander asked.

'Indeed we do,' the Englishman said.

Liberty nodded, said nothing.

'Good,' said the commander. 'Then we'll release you two immediately. Collect your weapons from my tent.'

'What about Billy the Kid?' asked Sinclair, pointing to the old man in the next cell. 'You can't leave him to rot in here.'

The commander shook his head and smiled.

'The old man's safer in here,' he said.

'Let me out of here,' the old man protested. 'I can fight as well as the next man.'

'You stay, old man,' the commander said. He unlocked the doors to Liberty's and the Englishman's cells.

'I can fight,' the old man insisted. 'I can show them redskins a thing or two.'

The commander simply ignored him.

47

'Why not release the old-timer?' Sinclair asked. 'What harm can it do?'

The commander shook his head. 'The moment he gets a chance he'll hightail it out of here and I can't spare the men to go after his damn fool hide again. He stays until this is all over. And that is final.'

'Sorry, old-timer,' Sinclair said. He stepped out of his cell, stretched and then smiled at the commander.

'Come on.' He motioned to Liberty.

CHAPTER SIX

Immediately they stepped outside the sound of an arrow hissed through the air and the commander was thrown backwards, an arrow having penetrated his left eye. The arrow had entered his eye cavity at an angle and pierced his brain. He died immediately.

'Don't think he'll be speaking to the captain after all,' Sinclair said.

The troopers both went down on their knees and raised their weapons but there didn't appear to be any target to aim at. The rain hammered the ground and made visibility poor but both men peered into the murky afternoon for the first sign of movement.

Liberty bent down to remove the commander's Colt from its holster and saw the jailhouse keys bulging from the officer's tunic pocket.

Quickly he palmed them and placed them into his own pocket.

'Hold your fire,' he said. 'That arrow didn't come from outside. One of more of them have breached the walls but save your ammunition until you see something.'

The troopers looked at him and both nodded. Lightning briefly illuminated the street and was followed by a loud rumbling of thunder. Rain hit the ground hard, pockmarking the dirt.

The Englishman ducked back into the relative safety of the jailhouse. He was not armed and it seemed a fool thing to be hanging around for a fight with no weapons at all with which to defend himself. When they returned his guns he'd be out in the thick of it but until then it made sense to keep the door between himself and any possible danger.

Suddenly men came from everywhere, both soldiers and civilians. Several arrows seemed to appear out of thin air, taking down three soldiers and one man who was dressed only in his underwear.

Liberty shot in the direction he imagined the arrows had come from but he knew it would be an amazing stroke of luck if he actually struck anything worth hitting. He looked up at the pigeon roosts and saw that none of them was manned. Where were the sentries?

'Is he. . . ?' Captain Roberts shouted over from a wagon behind which he was crouched; his meaning was perfectly clear.

'Yes,' Liberty shouted back. 'He's dead.'

'Where's the English guy?'

'In there,' Liberty yelled back, pointing to the jailhouse. 'There's at least four Indians inside the walls. I think they're somewhere by the saloon.'

Lightning flashed again and for the brief moment that the town was illuminated Liberty spotted an Indian, a Sioux, breaking cover from the side of the saloon and moving into the centre of the street. He shot quickly and had the satisfaction of seeing the Indian lifted off his feet and thrown backwards, dead before he hit the ground.

'Good shooting,' one of the troopers said, then found that he too had to shoot when an arrow flew perilously close to his head; thankfully it snapped harmlessly against the jailhouse wall.

'Where are they?' the captain yelled.

Liberty peered into the darkness. The rain had soaked him through and he had to push his hair back out of his eyes.

'I've got one of them,' he yelled. 'Judging from the way the arrows came I'd say there was another three, maybe four.'

'How'd they get past the sentries?' the captain yelled back. He looked up at the pigeon roosts.

51

They all appeared to be empty but he knew none of the men would have deserted their posts. The Indians must have somehow got to the three men, one in each roost, and killed them without anyone noticing. The savages, he reflected, were highly skilled fighters.

'Cover me,' Liberty said to the troopers; then he signalled to the captain, pointing to the hotel. He was going to make a break for it, feeling that if he made it he'd be able to spot the Indians and maybe trap them in a crossfire.

Liberty counted to three and then tore off across the street. He saw a muzzle flash come from the side of the saloon and he dived for the ground. He hit hard and rolled behind the town water pump. He came up immediately, fired and saw another Indian hit the ground, but now the Colt felt light in his hand; when he checked the chamber he saw that there was only the one bullet left.

'Damn!' he cursed.

'You've got another one,' the captain shouted. His words trailed off as an Indian landed on his back, having jumped from the building behind. The Indian rolled, pinning the captain beneath him, and brought his blade to the man's throat.

Liberty shot, taking the Indian square in the face, throwing him from the struggling captain in a mist of blood and gore.

The captain was stunned for a moment; he reached for his throat and felt the warm sticky blood. He had been cut but it didn't feel deep enough to prove fatal. He looked across at Liberty and saluted him; the damn Reb had saved his life.

'I'm out of shells,' Liberty yelled, waving the late commander's Colt about.

The captain popped several shells from his own belt and tossed them across to Liberty, who lay down prone and reached out for them. He moved back behind the water pump and filled the Colt's chamber.

'That's three down,' the captain yelled, directing his words towards Liberty. 'How many left?' His throat was bleeding heavily and although it wasn't life threatening he felt that if he didn't get it sewn up soon the wound could kill him after all.

Liberty held up his fist and popped one finger up and then shrugged his shoulders. He popped up another finger: *one, possibly two.*

'Cover me,' Liberty called and again broke into a run. He made one of the sentry posts just as an arrow flew uncomfortably close to his left shoulder. He grabbed the rope ladder and quickly pulled himself up, climbing for all he was worth towards the pigeon roost.

Gunfire and thunder seemed to be competing to drown each other out but then there came silence.

There did seem to be only the one Indian left in the town and for the moment he was hidden away, invisible.

Liberty reached the pigeon roost and saw the dead trooper curled on the floor of the wooden basket. The man's throat had been cut and then he had been scalped. The Indian intruders had, using the storm as cover, managed to breach the walls and somehow climb the rope ladders to reach pigeon roosts. Then they would have silently disposed of the guards: all this without being seen.

Liberty stood and peered into the darkness below, looking for the concealed Indian.

He could see nothing.

The sky rumbled again and Liberty took aim towards the side of the saloon where he was virtually sure the Indian was tucked away. He stood there, waiting for the next flash of lightning to light up the town. It came quickly and Liberty saw the Indian – and the Indian saw him. They made eye contact and the Indian seemed to know he was about to die. He smiled defiantly and closed his eyes.

Liberty fired three times in quick succession; the Indian was thrown backwards and out of the alleyway before hitting the ground.

'I've got him,' Liberty shouted; then when he turned and looked out over the town walls the night sky was lit up by the most brilliant flash of lightning he had ever seen. For the briefest of moments night became day and he saw hundreds upon hundreds of Indians sitting on horseback outside the walls. He knew too that this vast number was only a small section of those gathering in the hills.

Those others were about a quarter of a mile away, just sitting there, patiently waiting. The heavy rain didn't seem to bother them; even their horses were not worried by the fierce storm, remaining almost motionless. The warriors looked like ghosts against the distant skyline.

'There's a large war party outside,' he yelled down to the captain. 'The sentry's dead. Best get more men into these pigeon roosts straight away.'

The captain was on his feet, barking commands, all the while pressing a hand upon his throat to stem the flow of blood. He looked up at Liberty.

'You can come down now . . .' He paused, about to refer to Liberty once more as 'Reb', but he had a change of heart and instead mumbled: 'Well done.'

The captain wandered off in search of the doctor. If he didn't get the neck wound looked at immediately, before the Indians attacked again, the blood loss would make him too weak to fight.

CHAPTER SEVEN

'What now, English?' Liberty asked.

The night had passed without further attack but no one had managed any sleep. Everyone had kept their positions, not wanting to be taken by surprise again. It was a miserable watch with the storm continuing to rage until the first break of dawn. Only then with daylight had there been any respite and the town defenders had started assessing their losses. The dead soldiers were brought down from their pigeon roosts and then placed in the middle of the street, the commander alongside them. Each of them had been wrapped in an army issue blanket and placed in the livery stables for later burial.

By the time all this was done it was getting on for half past nine and already the sun was powerful. The ground, which had been soaked overnight, was once again baked solid.

'I'm in need of a soft bed,' Sinclair said. 'My back feels like it's broken.'

'Figures,' Liberty said wryly, but didn't explain what he meant by the crack. He still had the jailhouse keys in his pocket and, with the Englishman out of the way, he figured it would be an opportune time to visit the old-timer again. Maybe the sight of the keys would loosen the old man's tongue as to the reasons behind his insistence on leaving the relative safety of the town.

The Englishman frowned. 'I've still got a room in the hotel. Only room for one, I'm afraid, so I'll bid you farewell.'

'Sure,' Liberty said and sat himself down on the sidewalk. He made himself a quirly and watched the mêlée around him as he smoked. He ignored the Englishman and didn't look up when he heard him walk off, but his eyes followed him all the same. Again he wondered about the old man and his reasons for wanting to leave the town. Going out alone with so many hostile Indians in the hills equated to suicide.

It had to be something pretty damned important for the old man to be willing to run such a risk.

Something valuable enough to risk his life for.

A trooper galloped past, dust spitting up over Liberty. The trooper pulled his horse to a sudden stop, jumped down from the beast and immediately crouched into a defensive position. Then another man followed him, this time one of the town's residents, but the man reined his horse in heavy-handedly and he was thrown through the air, to come down painfully on the boardwalk outside the grain store.

Across the street the sergeant in charge of training the town's men, of moulding some sort of fighting force from amongst them, shook his head and made a gesture to the heavens with his arms, as if pleading with the Lord.

Liberty watched the proceedings and had to admit he didn't much fancy the town's chances. He thought of the Indians he had ridden past to get here and those he had seen watching the town during the storm.

They certainly made a formidable force.

A force too great against which to defend themselves and the townsfolk. Those Indians were seasoned warriors; all the town had was a small military force and a ragtag bunch of civilians, most of whom looked like farmers.

The Indians had used the chaos caused by the civil war to their advantage. While the whites were occupied in the great battles in the east, the tribes had started to take back some of the western lands stolen from them; where Indians had once seemed beaten by the might of the American soldiers they had risen up, stood tall again and looked to their leaders to lead them into war. The previous year the Indian wars had intensified with the Battle of the River Platte and hostilities had been frequent and progressively bloodier ever since.

Liberty stood up and walked back to the saloon. He was in need of a wash-up and was sure the establishment would offer such facilities. There was so much trail dust on him that it felt like an outer skin. He noticed that Captain Roberts, the nasty gash on his throat held together by rough stitching, was looking at him as he crossed the street but he ignored him. He pushed through the saloon batwings and made straight for the counter. He had the feeling that he and the burly captain had come to some sort of understanding.

Liberty had a drink while he waited for the saloon girl to ready his tub in the back room, but before his drink had even settled in his stomach the warning bugle sounded.

The Indians were attacking again.

'I'll be back for the bath,' Liberty said to the barkeep; he tossed a coin on to the counter. 'Make sure the water stays warm.'

Once outside Liberty pulled his Colt from its holster and started across the street to join the men at the walls. He stopped dead in his tracks when he noticed the Englishman in the alley beside the jailhouse. He was standing on an upturned barrel, which he had no doubt dragged over to the jailhouse wall. He was talking to the old man through the bars in the window.

'English,' Liberty shouted. 'You coming?'

The Englishman frowned at Liberty, shrugged his shoulders and then went back to his conversation with the old man. All around them gunfire sounded. A man fell from the upper walls, an arrow sticking out from his chest, and crashed through the floor of a wagon. The team reared up as the frightened animals tried to free themselves from their reins.

Sleep in a soft bed. Liberty smiled grimly. The dirty lying Englishman had wanted to get to the old man and find out what it was that he was so willing to risk his life for.

'Devious son of a bitch,' Liberty muttered. He walked into the alley and kicked the barrel with such force that the Englishman lost his balance and fell head first to the ground.

The Englishman came to his feet almost instantly. He took a jab at Liberty but the American ducked, easily avoiding the blow while delivering an uppercut. It took the Englishman under the chin and sent him reeling backwards.

The Englishman managed to keep his footing and instantly he came back at Liberty. This time he was far more effective, delivering several well-placed blows that culminated in the American falling back on to the ground.

Liberty felt as if there was a thunderstorm within his head and he had to give the Englishman credit. He had a vicious punch on him and had used his fists with considerable skill, moving like a prize fighter. Liberty was about to get back to his feet when dust kicked up from the ground besides him.

An arrow furrowed the dirt, barely inches from his head. Then the sun itself was eclipsed as flaming arrow upon flaming arrow filled the sky. Falling like hailstones they landed in the ground, in the sides of buildings and, in several instances, into warm soft flesh. The deadly storm continued and Liberty's fight with the Englishman didn't seem to matter any longer.

'We'd best settle our differences later,' Sinclair said and helped the fallen man to his feet.

'I'll be watching you from now on,' Liberty snarled, rubbing his aching jaw. 'From now on where you go, I follow.'

'Heaven forbid!' The Englishman smiled.

The two men ran out into the street and were greeted by absolute chaos. The captain spotted them and waved them over.

'You men get to the wall and get shooting,' he yelled.

61

'I'm beginning to regret that fact that that Indian didn't manage to slit the captain's throat just a little deeper.' Sinclair looked at Liberty, noticing with some satisfaction that the American had an angry-looking welt forming upon his chin.

'Watch out,' Liberty yelled, pushing the Englishman aside as a hail of deadly arrows came down around them.

'Frightfully kind of you, old boy.' Sinclair increased his speed and sprinted across the street to the town walls. Once there he located a slit and peered through; almost immediately he fired his weapon and saw another Indian fall from a hand-some-looking appaloosa.

Liberty was soon beside him, his own weapon in his hand. Above them rifle fire sounded from the pigeon roosts, while other men occupied the ledge that had been constructed towards the top of the defensive walls. A moment later one of those men fell, hitting the ground beside Liberty. The man was beyond help: that much was obvious. He had been dead even before he hit the ground, his face blown away by a direct hit from a high-calibre rifle.

CHAPTER EIGHT

Yet another body fell from above them and landed hard on the ground.

Liberty pulled away from the slit he'd been firing through and looked up. He noticed that the ledge that had been constructed close to the top of the wall for the defenders to stand on was looking distinctly bare. Moments ago there had been at least twelve men up there; now he could only see six.

'I'm going up there,' he said to the Englishman, who was firing shot after shot through one of the slits.

There were at least a couple of hundred Indians outside and they were attacking with a new ferocity, trying to grind the town's defenders down. Far from fighting like mindless savages they seemed to have a well-planned strategy. Once this attack was over the surviving Indians would ride away and, before the town's defenders could recover, a new band of warriors would turn up to continue the onslaught. The attacks would grow more and more frequent, giving the town's defenders no respite, no relief from the relentless wave of violence.

'Well, enjoy yourself,' Sinclair said, then he ducked just in time. A flaming arrow came whizzing through the slit he'd been looking through and buried itself in the chuck wagon. The canvas immediately caught fire, the flames spreading with a ferocious speed. The cook ran across and entered the inferno; he threw as many supplies out on to the ground as he could manage before the heat forced him to jump back out. There was no hope of saving the wagon itself. All the cook could do was release the terrified team from their traces; the horses immediately started to gallop around within the walled town, causing even more danger to the defenders within the walls.

'Get those damn horses under control,' the captain said. A moment later he had to shoot a particularly good-looking animal that had come galloping towards him, terror in the poor beast's eyes. The horse went down immediately and the captain felt a pang of genuine sorrow.

'These Indians are damn fine shots,' Sinclair remarked; then he stood up quickly and fired off several shots into the chaos outside.

Liberty, running to a ladder, saw the captain watching him from his position up the street. He gave a gesture, almost a salute, and started up the ladder. He reached the top quickly, jumped on to the ledge and looked down on to a scene that equalled in its horror the most terrible brutal battles he had seen during the War Between the States.

The Indians were attacking on all flanks, battering the hastily constructed town walls with rocks, arrows and tomahawks. There were many more of them than he'd been able to see through the slit in the walls: maybe five hundred out there. A few of the Indians had rifles and he watched as a brave stopped his horse and worked the lever of what looked like a Spencer, sending a bullet into the breech.

Liberty fired before the brave could aim and the man toppled backwards off his horse. A trickle of blood ran from the hole in his throat where the slug had passed through, obliterating his Adam's apple and mangling his windpipe.

'Good shooting,' the man to Liberty's left said. He was a balding civilian in his mid-fifties. He held a gleaming new Winchester and Liberty wondered if he could shoot with it and actually hit anything. There was no time to find out, though, as Liberty noticed a brave starting to scale the walls with the aid of a rope he had succeeded in lassooing over the top of the wall.

Liberty ran to the rope and cut it with his knife, sending the brave falling to the ground. There was no sense in wasting a bullet; the fall would at the very least have severely injured the brave and most likely have killed him. Either way it wasn't important; it was putting him out of the fight that really mattered.

Liberty looked down. He couldn't see the brave move but then the body jerked as someone cruelly put a bullet into him for good measure. Liberty had to duck to avoid yet another flight of burning arrows that whizzed into the town. He sprang up again, firing his Colt, then he crouched down again on the ledge while he reloaded his weapon.

The battle continued and although the Indians were receiving heavy casualties they kept up their onslaught. Bullets screamed from the town, some finding targets but most powering uselessly into the ground. Wave after wave of arrows flew through the air, landing in the roofs and walls of the buildings. Dozen of fires broke out as the wood caught and Liberty noticed that the saloon had become a raging inferno. The fire had started inside, an arrow having gone through a window, and now it was out of control. The sound of bottles exploding inside and glasses smashing could be heard quite clearly.

There could be no saving the building; absurdly, all Liberty could think of was his bath, the water now likely boiling away to steam inside the burning building.

'Hold your fire,' Liberty shouted, waving to the captain who was firing through the slits in the large gates, but he didn't seem to hear, or notice his gestures. Liberty cursed. He ran back to a ladder and quickly made his way down it.

He slid down the last foot or so and hit the ground running. He sped across to the captain and pulled him by the shoulder, spinning him around.

'Tell your men to hold their fire,' he gasped.

'What?' Captain Roberts looked him up and down. 'Are you loco?'

'They are trying to exhaust your ammunition before the main attack,' Liberty said. 'You'd be better off fighting these fires.'

The captain considered this for a moment.

'You may be right,' he acknowledged.

He signalled for the bugler to sound the cease fire. He looked around him at the town; several of the buildings were on fire but most could be saved with swift action. The saloon, though, was beyond help; the flames were so high that if the wind changed suddenly the fire would make the leap to the town walls. If that happened they would be beaten.

The portly sergeant ran over to them. He was holding a smoking Colt Dragoon and he glanced at Liberty suspiciously. He looked at his commanding officer for an explanation.

'Get a fire-fighting detail together,' the captain ordered. 'And tell the other sergeant to fetch the dynamite. Now may be the time to give some to those red devils.'

'You've got dynamite?' Liberty looked at the man dumbfounded. Dynamite would considerably even things up and might have even saved some of the lives already lost.

'A little.' The captain nodded. 'Just a little. I was keeping it until using it became imperative. As you say, we need to stop this now. Concentrate on the fires.'

Liberty wasn't going to argue with that.

A moment later the second sergeant turned up with six sticks of dynamite. He was panting heavily and his uniform showed thick sweat patches across his chest and beneath his arms.

'Is that all you've got?' Liberty asked.

'Afraid so,' Roberts said. 'Now you see why I didn't want to use it.'

'Sure,' Liberty said. 'Give me two sticks.'

He took the dynamite and ran to the ladder. Quickly he climbed back up to the ledge. There were two men either side of him and he told them to resume firing while he crouched down, capped the dynamite's fuses to three seconds each and lit the first stick with a sulphur match.

He stood up quickly and threw the dynamite into a group of Indians who were sending arrows soaring into the sky. The dynamite landed in the middle of the group and immediately exploded, sending a deathly cloud of smoke, blood and gore over the battlefield. He threw the second stick towards another group of Indians, maybe twenty men, who were once again lighting their coal-oil tipped arrows ready to fire into the town.

The explosion tore them apart limb from limb. Blood splattered on the air and landed like rain on the warriors still battling to overwhelm the town. A crimson gore soaked them.

Chayton screamed out for his braves to retreat.

He hadn't been expecting this. The small army unit was better armed than he'd thought. He looked at the hellish scene before him and knew that the explosions had cost the lives of many braves. Add those to the men who had already fallen and it had been a costly battle.

This was bad medicine.

His visions had warned of defeat but until now he couldn't see how that could happen.

He howled again, waving his lance frantically, calling his braves back to him. They would retreat for the moment, retire to the safety of the camp and plan their next attack. If the white men had dynamite then his braves would have to be far more cautious in their approach. He wondered how much of the explosive the white men had and couldn't understand why they had waited until now to use it. The whites were sly, like the coyote, and could strike with the viciousness of the grizzly bear. The dynamite was deadly effective and had turned the course of the battle.

Until the first explosion the chief had been confident that the town would fall before long. Now he was not too sure and he was not going to waste his men against the white man's explosives. This called for a suspension of their attack while they reassessed the situation.

He turned his horse and sent it into a gallop. He heard the braves tearing along behind him, leaving the dead and the wounded on the battlefield behind to the gods and the fates. Once they had covered some distance and were out of sight of the town he pulled his horse to a stop; his braves did likewise. He looked around at their puzzled expressions as they looked towards him for further orders.

'Bad medicine,' he said. 'We will return and bring good medicine with us.'

CHAPTER NINE

Liberty joined in as the buckets of water were passed along several lines of people, each tackling one of the many fires. He noticed the Englishman at the front of his particular line. That was good; he liked to know where the Englishman was; that knowledge allowed Liberty to concentrate fully on the matter at hand.

The buckets, filled with water from the well at the centre of main street, were passed along as quickly as possible, water sloshing over their brims. All across the town this scene was repeated as men, women and children did their bit to control the fires that were licking at several buildings. Every person in town joined in the fight against the fires. Even the men manning the sentry posts were now in line, the likelihood of further Indian attacks seemingly forgotten as the very real current danger was confronted.

The captain shouted out orders and the portly sergeant looked disgruntled to find himself at the head of one line, passing the buckets along, rather than taking a more fitting role and taking the fight to the enemy. With the exception of the saloon, which was beyond help, every fire was tackled and extinguished. Everyone worked as a team, all movement coordinated as gallon after gallon of water was thrown on to the flames.

Afterwards Liberty fell to the ground and lay there for a moment, exhausted. He closed his eyes and listened to the activity around him as people regrouped and once more assessed their losses. When he opened his eyes again the Englishman was standing over him.

'Well, you seem to be the hero of the hour,' Sinclair said. 'Jolly well done with the explosives, old boy.'

Liberty stood up and wiped himself down. He saw the captain surveying the damage to the town and, ignoring the Englishman, he got up and walked over to him.

'How much more do you think you can take?' Liberty asked, speaking directly to the captain. 'Everyone here is exhausted, some seem to be on the brink of snapping. I've seen people like this before and soon many people will tip over into madness. And all for this crummy little town. Maybe you should seriously think of arranging a retreat.'

Captain Roberts looked at him for a moment before speaking.

'This town must be defended at all costs,' he said. 'We'll take whatever is thrown at us but we will endure.' He rubbed a hand gently over his throat, checking that no stitches had split during the action.

'You're losing more and more men with each fresh attack,' Liberty pointed out. 'If we don't make a run for it you'll have the death of all these people on your hands.'

'Reinforcements will arrive in less than a week. We'll drive these red devils back into the mountains if it is the last thing we do.'

'I don't think you can hold out more than another day.'

'You're an expert on such matters?' The captain seemed to have a grudging respect for the Southerner but he was clearly tired and in some pain. He did not intend to debate the matter. He had his orders and that was all there was to it.

'I know a futile situation when I see one,' Liberty said, and he cast a downward look as his mind's eye gazed into the past.

He had lived a violent existence: death and destruction had seemed to follow him around. He had been born amidst violence, his mother giving birth from the back of a wagon while Indians attacked. The baby that would become the man had hardly taken his first breath before being introduced to the brutal savagery of the world. It seemed to Liberty that ever since that day savagery had been a constant companion, waiting, goading. There had never been any real peace in Liberty's life. The grim reaper seemed always to have been at his side: death tagging along for the ride.

'Maybe,' Roberts said. 'You did well. You have courage and are a good man. With more like you we could give these Indians a whipping they'd never forget.'

Liberty smiled, thinking that not too long ago this man would have been the enemy; now they were united. Pity the captain had almost had to get his gizzard cut to reach this state of affairs.

'I do what it takes to stay alive,' he said. 'That's all I've ever done.'

'What do you think happens next?' The captain looked at Liberty. It was evident from his eyes that all the bravado had gone from the man. He was putting his trust in Liberty.

'The dynamite scared them some and they don't know we've only four sticks left,' Liberty said. 'They'll take that as bad medicine and it may delay their next attack but they will return. They're trying to grind us down little by little.'

'We need to hold out until the reinforcements get here,' the captain insisted. 'We are Americans, we are soldiers, and American soldiers do not flee from a fight. Like the men who defended the Alamo we must remain steadfast.'

Liberty shook his head.

'The Alamo was under siege for thirteen days,' he said. 'I don't think we'll last thirteen hours.'

'I pray you are wrong,' the captain said. He turned his eyes away from the Southerner, scanning the townsfolk in the street. To a man they all looked to be on their last legs.

'There may be something we could do,' Liberty said, thoughtfully.

'What do you suggest?'

'Take the fight to them,' Liberty said. 'The surprise will throw them and if we can get their leader they'll think the great spirit is displeased and that all medicine will be bad for them. Take out the leader and it's over.'

'How do you propose we do that?' The captain smiled despite gravity of the situation. 'There's thousands of the red devils out there and our numbers are diminishing fast.'

'What we need is a marksman with a long-range rifle,' Liberty said.

The captain nodded. He called a trooper over.

'Lawrence, tell him about your baby.'

The trooper knew exactly what his superior was referring to. He smiled proudly and held up his rifle.

'It's a Schroeder, fifty-three-calibre,' he said. 'It's got a range of around a mile on a good day.'

'Can you hit something that far away?' Liberty asked.

'I've done it before,' the trooper said. 'The Indians call this weapon "the gun that fires today and kills tomorrow". They believe the bullet continues travelling until it finds a target.'

'And they are not wrong.' The captain laughed and patted the trooper on the back.

'Then I say a few of us sneak out, get as close to the Indian camp as possible,' Liberty said. He started to roll himself a quirly. 'I know Indians and, like I say, if we take out the leader or even their medicine man the battle's over. They may be planning another night attack, so they won't expect us to be coming at them. The element of surprise could provide us with an advantage – and we sure do need an advantage.'

The captain remained silent for several long moments; then he nodded.

'When?' he asked.

'After dark,' Liberty said. 'This man and his rifle, myself and maybe two other men. I'll select them.

And I'll take two more sticks of that dynamite.'

'As you wish,' the captain said. 'And – I never thought I'd say this to a Reb – but may God be with you.'

'Ain't that something?' Liberty said with a smile. 'A Blue Belly with heart!'

CHAPTER TEN

Night brought an uneasy peace to the town of Red Rock.

Liberty, Trooper Lawrence, the Englishman, and two other troopers selected because they were the best shots among the ranks, left the town by dropping down over the walls with ropes, which were quickly pulled back up after them. Several men were stationed on the ledge, ready to throw the ropes over the wall again or open the gates, depending on the situation when they returned. If there were too many Indians in pursuit and it was deemed too risky to open the gates – for it took precious seconds to close them again – then the five men would have to fend for themselves. That much was understood by each of the men.

The landscape immediately outside the town was flat but there were irrigation ditches that provided natural cover. The ditches ran across terrain that was strewn with large boulders that had fallen over time from the mountains that bordered the small valley in which the town had been constructed.

'We need to get to that ditch yonder as quickly as possible,' Liberty said. 'But we also need to move silently and keep to the shadows of the walls.'

'You're not asking much,' Sinclair quipped.

'This is no time for jokes,' Liberty said. 'If there are Indians out there on watch, which there must be, they'll have the ears and eyes of hawks.'

'Then lead the way,' the Englishman said.

Lawrence grunted as he threw his precious rifle over his back. Authority for this mission had been ceded to Liberty, since it was he who had selected the men for this foolhardy endeavour. The marksman and the soldiers had been picked for their expertise, but the Englishman was with them so that Liberty could keep an eye on him. For the moment Liberty was fully focused on turning the tide against the Indians but, all the same, he'd rather have the Englishman where he could see him.

They moved slowly to the south, keeping close to the town walls and the shadows they threw out across the ground. There was a pale moon in the sky but thankfully there was some cloud cover to hide its full brightness.

They reached the first irrigation ditch without incident and one by one they jumped down into it.

Liberty called them to an immediate halt as soon as he had lowered himself over the edge. He was the last one into the ditch, which was about eight feet deep, but the walls had been dug out of jagged soil and there were plenty of hand- and footholds to aid climbing out again.

'When we reach the far side of this ditch,' he said, 'we need to stay silent. The Indians will have sentries about and if they are planning a night attack we could run straight into them.'

'You mean there are Indians out there?' the Englishman joshed but everyone ignored him.

'Let's just get close enough to get a shot with this.' Lawrence indicated the rifle slung over his shoulder. It was certainly a handsome-looking weapon, its brass fittings gleaming in the moonlight. It was breech-loading, which made it much quicker to reload and fire than the older muzzle-loading variety that it had replaced. Unlike the cumbersome muzzle-loaders the action of the bolt meant the weapon could be reloaded while the man firing it was lying down, which made the chances of keeping your head on your shoulders between shots that much better.

'Follow my lead,' Liberty said. 'Slow and easy. Those Indians could hear a fart in a thunderstorm.'

'You have a colourful turn of phrase,' Sinclair said as he followed behind Liberty. Lawrence followed directly after him and the two remaining troopers took up the rear.

An owl hooted in the distance and Liberty held up a hand for the party to halt. He strained his ears to pick up any further sounds, knowing the Indians would often mimic animal sounds to pass messages to one another. The owl hooted again and Liberty felt reasonably confident that it was an actual bird and not some Indian sentry.

'Come on,' he said and once again they walked slowly towards the far side of the irrigation ditch.

It took them perhaps ten minutes to cover the breadth of the ditch and it was now that their mission became really dangerous. They had to climb out of the ditch and make a break for the hills. They would have to cover maybe forty or fifty feet out in the open, exposed and easy pickings for any Indian who happened to spot them.

'One at a time,' Liberty said. 'When we get on to level ground, keep low. Lie prone and snipe towards the hill. I'll go first.'

The Englishman leant his back against the ditch wall and cupped his hands at waist-height to form a step up for Liberty.

'Obliged,' Liberty said and took the step. He reached for the top of the ditch and pulled himself up and on to the hard ground. He lay there for a moment, his eyes scanning the darkness, but all was silently still.

'Next one,' he said. He reached over the edge of the ditch to give the Englishman a hand up. Each man similarly helped the next until all five of them lay on the ground.

'Weapons cocked and ready.' Liberty drew one of his Colts and cocked the hammer.

He started to crawl forward, followed by the others, towards the cover of the hills. Again luck was with them and they reached these without incident, though twice they had to stop and listen when some strange night sound broke the silence. They hunkered behind a huge boulder that jutted out of the baked ground to a height of maybe twenty feet or more.

'Now it gets mighty hot,' Liberty said. 'We're close to their camp.'

'Quiet.' Sinclair held a hand up for silence. He cocked his pistol. 'I thought I heard something then.'

They remained silent, listening, but other than the usual night sounds there was nothing to be heard. They were just about to move out when the sound of voices forced them to freeze. This time there was no mistaking the sound. They had heard two Indian voices.

Liberty peered around the rock and spotted two Indians on a bluff about twenty feet above them and to the left. They had their backs to him and were seated on a stump of an old tree; they were speaking in hushed voices. They were sentries, no doubt, but they had obviously not been expecting anyone to be wandering about and they had become unwary. Liberty pulled his Bowie from its sheath and looked at the other men.

'We'll have to take these two out silently,' he whispered the words. 'Anyone else confident in using a blade?'

One of the troopers came forward, a young man, barely twenty years of age. He had a vicious-looking military-issue dagger.

Liberty looked at the trooper, then nodded.

'Have to get up behind them,' he said. 'Hand over the mouth and slit the throat. Don't hesitate. If they raise the alarm we're finished.'

The trooper nodded. He had about him a confidence that belied his youth and he signalled with a wave of his dagger.

'Come on,' Liberty said. 'The rest of you stay here until we signal.'

The two Indians, engrossed in their conversation, were taken by total surprise when Liberty and the young trooper came up behind them and quickly put hands over their mouths to stifle any cries. Then they pulled the two sentries backwards and brought their blades to their throats. Both braves died quickly and Liberty and the trooper lowered them gently to the ground.

Liberty turned and waved for the others to follow.

They continued upwards without further incident until they reached a vantage point that allowed them to see down into the Indian village below. Each of them, to a man, gasped. They had known the Indians were here in force but no one had realized the sheer numbers. Below them, in the flatlands, they could see the temporary village that the Indians had constructed. Tepee upon tepee stretched out into the distance and there was a large makeshift corral that took up maybe four acres and contained many horses.

Indians could be seen huddled together in small bands around their campfires, of which there were too many to be counted as they twinkled away in the darkness. Such was the size of the gathering that the Indians furthest away showed merely as small movements, almost a whisper of the wind, in the blackness of the night.

'It's Armageddon,' Liberty said.

'I think every Indian in America's down there,' Sinclair cracked.

'I've never seen so many,' Liberty said. Even from

here he could see they were made up of numerous tribes. He could clearly make out a tall brave wearing a Comanche headdress, another wore Apache feathers and there were Sioux and braves from tribes he didn't recognize.

It didn't bode well: the Comanche and the Apache were bitter enemies for a start, and the fact that they seemed to have settled their differences and joined forces to defeat a common enemy had terrifying implications. Natives of other tribes who usually wouldn't breathe the same air as one another were milling about amongst the vast Indian encampment.

'Can you see their leader?' Lawrence asked, itching to demonstrate the abilities of his rifle. He was sure he could pick a target off cleanly from this distance. The weapon's sights were such that it wouldn't present much of a challenge at all. The difficult thing was selecting a target to deliver the bad medicine with the maximum effect.

All five men hugged the ground and stared at the awe-inspiring sight below them. Had there ever been such a large gathering of tribes any other time in history?

'I've never seen anything like this,' Liberty said. He had been forced to flee from a large war party when he'd arrived at Red Rock but this was something else entirely. He estimated there could be as many as five thousand Indians down there.

'We've got no chance of picking off anyone important,' Sinclair opined.

Liberty had to agree. The nearest point of the great camp was just short of half a mile away but the furthest point they could see was more than a mile away. There was no doubt that it went on beyond that.

This was a big country and the Indians were filling it.

'A million-to-one chance,' Liberty said.

'So what do we do?' Lawrence asked. The rifle was feeling heavy in his arms. It seemed a pity to come all this way and not send some sort of message to the murderous redskins.

'We'll wait a little while,' Liberty said. 'You never know; we may strike lucky. If not we'll sneak back to town.'

'At least we know what we're up against,' Sinclair said. 'This information could convince the captain that we may have to cut and run if we're to have any chance.'

'The reinforcements can't be far off,' the younger of the other two troopers said. 'They're carrying two Gatling guns. I reckon then we'd be a match for even all these Indians.'

'Maybe,' Liberty said. 'But they'll have to be pretty damn quick.' He had seen the guns in action during the war and was well aware of the carnage they could cause but they were prone to overheat and jam. Even if they got here before the Indians completely overran the town, victory was no sure thing.

Liberty was about to suggest heading back to the town when a burst of movement from the edges of the Indian gathering caught his eye. There was a trail of men all heading for the corral; others had formed a line and were doing a war dance while other men mounted horses and rode through the middle.

'They're sending out a war party,' Liberty said. He pulled the sticks of dynamite from his shirt. He capped them with a long fuse. Sinclair peered over a rock, straining his eyes.

'There's maybe a hundred mounted,' he reported.

'And they can afford to lose each and every man,' Liberty said. 'They can send war parties of that size out till Christmas.'

'Give me a target,' Lawrence said, 'and I'll take him out.'

'Wait until we can select a suitable target,' Liberty said. 'As soon as the rifle sounds, the rest of you fire at the Indians. They'll come in pursuit and I'll light the dynamite. It's got a long fuse. Should slow them down.'

'And we hightail it back to town, I take it?' Sinclair said.

'Yep,' Liberty replied, then, with a shrug of his shoulders, 'It's as good a plan as any.'

They didn't have to wait long. Soon a large man kicked a pure-white horse forward and rode to the front of the war party. He raised a hand and addressed the warriors he would lead. He was a chief. That was obvious.

'Can you hit him from here?' Liberty looked at Lawrence.

'I sure can,' the trooper answered. He took aim. He took in a deep breath and mumbled to his weapon. Then he pulled the trigger and all hell broke loose.

Liberty saw the Indian thrown from his horse which spooked the other horses and some kicked out, striking men, breaking flesh and bones while others bucked their riders from their backs.

'Now fire,' Liberty yelled, and as the other troopers started shooting he struck a sulphur match against a rock. He took a flame to the first stick of dynamite and then the other. Gunfire deafened him; he yelled for the men to skedaddle back to town, then started back down the banking himself. They had to get back to the ditch before the dynamite went up if they were to have any hope of reaching the town in one piece. They had taken the

89

Indians by surprise but their advantage would be short-lived and the Indians would soon respond with deadly force.

They reached the ditch and one by one they jumped in. They started moving immediately, running along the ditch in the direction of town. Each of them felt the ground shake beneath their feet as the first stick of dynamite exploded. The second stick exploded moments later but by then their eardrums had taken a battering and it seemed to go off with only a dull thud.

They gained the far side of the ditch and climbed out as quickly as possible. They sprinted for the town gates, waving to the sentries as they came. They were no Indians in sight, so the big gates were pulled open and closed again quickly once all the men were inside.

'Did you get the chief?' Captain Roberts looked down at the raiders. All of them were seated on the ground, panting for breath.

'We got a chief,' Liberty said. 'I don't think they'll attack again tonight. Not now we've given them some bad medicine. But they'll be back soon enough.'

'There are more Indians out there than you'd believe,' Sinclair said.

'How many?' The captain looked at each of the men in turn but none of them was prepared to make an estimate. In the end it was Liberty who spoke.

'I saw some big armies during the war,' he said. 'But those Indians have more men out there than I've ever seen in one place.'

'Then we have our work cut out,' the captain replied. He produced a cigar from his tunic, struck a match on a boot heel and sucked the tobacco into life.

'The Indians will regroup and mount a fresh attack,' Liberty said. 'And I intend to get some sleep before that happens.'

Chayton stood there, the moonlight caressing his finely sculpted features, highlighting his handsome head and illuminating his eyes. He was troubled: he hadn't expected the whites to launch a counter attack against his forces. The men within the town were getting bolder and the fire sticks they had left behind had claimed several of his braves. The whites had also managed to kill the Lakota chief, Little Tree. They had shot from the concealment of the night, using a weapon with incredible range and Chayton was aware that such a weapon would prove dangerous. From now on they would have constantly to be on their guard, would have to consider the possibility that the whites could have a man out there, concealed anywhere on the boulder-strewn terrain, with a rifle that could bring sudden death from incredible distances.

He knew the army reinforcements would be racing towards the town of Red Rock. He wondered if the men he had sent out had met with the army yet. Wondered how the battle had gone. Had the small force he had sent out been triumphant or had the white man's army bested them? There was no way of knowing and the Indian was wise enough to realize that his warriors had to take the town as soon as possible, before any white reinforcements arrived and helped turn the tables in favour of the town.

He stood there for some time, listening to the sounds of the night before turning on his heel and heading back to the main camp. Soon it would be a good time to die: the Indian chief was ready if death was indeed intended for him. His vision, though, had told him he would survive, that he would live to see the day when his people would once again prosper and live in a land free of the white invaders.

CHAPTER ELEVEN

Liberty was offered a bed in the livery stable, which had been converted into a crude barracks for the soldiers, but he chose to stay outside and made himself comfortable on the wooden bench just outside the jailhouse. It suited him here. He would be ready for any night-time attacks the Indians cared to launch and he could see pretty much everything that went on in town. He still had the jailhouse keys in his pocket and the mystery over the old man's intentions had him mightily puzzled.

He had questioned the Englishman earlier, wanting to know what it was he had been discussing with the old man when he had come across him just before the most recent Indian attack. But Sinclair had merely shrugged his shoulders and said that he had been rudely interrupted before he could really get into a conversation, said that he had just been passing the time of day with the old-timer.

Liberty didn't believe the Englishman and he certainly didn't trust him. It was plain that Lord Sinclair was set on discovering the old man's secret.

That made two of them.

The fact that the old man had repeatedly tried to leave town despite the great danger outside the fortified walls was troubling; it was a wonder the army hadn't been more interested in the old man's reasoning behind his apparent death wish. But then, he supposed, the army's concerns were more with the Indian threat. They certainly didn't trust the old man and although they needed every available finger on a trigger they refused to release him. They were obviously pretty sure that he'd try and vamoose again as soon as their backs were turned.

The Englishman also had been curious as to the old-timer's thinking. That much had been evident from the look in Sinclair's eyes, and no matter what he said it was plain to see that he too was interested in the old man and whatever might be his reason for wanting to flee the town at the first opportunity.

It had to be something mighty important.

It was something that Liberty meant to discover.

He looked up and down the street. There were still three sentry posts standing and each was manned, men taking it in turns, four hours at a time. There were also two armed men at the town gates. Slipping into the jailhouse unseen would be difficult and Liberty didn't want to push his luck with Captain Roberts. The death of the commander had severely altered the military power structure in town and falling foul of Roberts was to be avoided. Liberty felt that they seemed to have built a level of understanding between them but one wrong move could put the captain back on the defensive.

Liberty reached into his shirt and took out the makings. He quickly made himself a quirly and sucked the smoke to life. He sat there, listening to the night sounds. Far away an owl hooted, followed by another and then what sounded like the howl of a coyote. He smiled, knowing that this time the sounds were the Indians communicating. He couldn't understand what they meant but he knew enough about them to recognize the sounds for what they were. The raiding party had hit the Indians hard with their surprise attack and, although he couldn't be sure, he expected that the last sticks of dynamite had taken out several of the pursuing Indians who were unlucky enough to have been near the stuff when it went off.

A soldier walked past and nodded his head at Liberty, who tipped his hat in reply. He watched the trooper walk down the street towards the livery stables-cum-barracks. Liberty finished his smoke and flicked it on to the ground, where it burst into a shower of sparks before winking away to nothing.

He lay back and brought his hat down over his eyes. It had been a long day and he was dog-tired. He'd take a little shut-eye but even in rest he would stay alert, half of him remaining aware of everything happening around him even during the deepest of sleeps.

It was a skill he had learned long ago.

The Englishman parted the thick cloth that passed for curtains and peered across the street towards the jailhouse. He could see the dumb American stretched out on the bench. His head was tipped forward, his hat covering his eyes, but the Englishman didn't think he was sleeping.

This wasn't good, not good at all. The Englishman had planned on sneaking back to the jailhouse and having another go at the old man. He had a hunch about him and his reasons for wanting to escape from the town: a hunch that told him there was money involved – a lot of money. There were only two things that could make a man risk everything he had: romance and money. He didn't think the old man would be interested in the former, except maybe with his horse, so it had to be hard cash: gold even. The old-timer was too old for love and in dire need of the other, the Englishman thought.

'Damn your American hide!' the Englishman said, staring through the window at Liberty. Getting into the jailhouse unseen would be difficult enough with the army about but nigh on impossible with the American bedded down on the bench: a slumbering sentry, set directly to the left of the one and only door. He supposed he should go to bed and get some rest before the inevitable madness started again but he couldn't sleep with all this on his mind. The mystery of the old man tormented him; his mind was far too active for any chance of real rest.

As it turned out Sinclair did manage to snatch a hour or so's sleep, but he was soon awake again and he went immediately to the window to check whether the American was still out there. It was no surprise to discover that Liberty was indeed still there, snoozing on the bench outside the jailhouse.

The night was particularly clear, a huge moon hung in a dark-blue star-studded sky as if painted there by a child. It illuminated the surrounding land and gave off a glow that seemed both ethereal and eerie. In the distance, above the hills, the Englishman saw a shooting star; he watched its progress as it streaked through the heavens to vanish into the nothingness of infinity.

He took one last look at Liberty. The man hadn't moved an inch, so Sinclair quietly went out into the hallway. He stood still for a moment, listening for the sound of any of the other hotel guests but he was greeted with silence. He walked the length of the passageway and quietly made his way downstairs. Once there he went to the rear of the building and let himself out on to the street.

CHAPTER TWELVE

Liberty opened his eyes. For a moment he was disoriented, unsure of what it was that had awoken him, but then he heard it again: the sound of an arrow whistling through the air. He rolled off the bench, pulled his Colt from leather and looked around, assessing the situation.

Once again the Indians were attacking.

He hadn't expected this.

Not so soon.

The savages were maintaining their tactics of trying to grind the town's defenders down, depriving them of any respite from the madness of battle. It was as much a psychological war as it was physical and the strain was beginning to tell; soldiers and the makeshift militia collided in the street as they made their way to their posts. Faces looked battle-weary, stunned, vacant even. Liberty had seen faces like this before, during the war between the North and South and he knew that the faces he had seen back then and the faces he saw now had much in common. They were those of men close to breaking point, heading towards a kind of insanity.

'Hold your fire until you see a target,' Liberty shouted. Once again he ran to the town walls. He noticed Captain Roberts crossing the street, buttoning his tunic as he hurried along.

'Damn and blast!' the captain yelled. 'Damn and blast those Indians!'

There was silence for a moment, then the sound of another arrow whistling over the town was followed by several bursts of wild shooting. Bullets screamed off into the semi-darkness in their search for an unseen target.

'Hold your fire,' Liberty shouted again. 'They're playing with us.'

Captain Roberts glared at Liberty but said nothing. He came over to him and looked down his nose at the Southerner.

'I wasn't aware you had been put in charge, Reb,' he said.

'The Indians are hoping we'll use up all our ammunition,' Liberty said. 'They're trying to weaken us in stages.'

'I'm well aware of the workings of the savage mind,' the captain said. 'I've fought Indians in the past and I'll fight them again in the future.'

'Yes, sir,' Liberty said, feeling it prudent to show a little respect to the officer. Faked respect it may have been but the situation demanded keeping on the right side of the self-important son of a bitch. It seemed that the captain's earlier softened attitude towards Liberty had vanished.

Captain Roberts turned and addressed the soldiers and the militia:

'Fire only when you see a target,' he shouted. Then he turned back to Liberty. 'Now remember, Reb, I'm in charge here.'

'Yes sir,' Liberty said with what he hoped sounded like sincere respect.

'Can I help you two gentlemen?'

Liberty looked at the Englishman. He was fully dressed and didn't look at all as though he had just been rudely awakened from sleep. He really was the oddest man Liberty had ever come across.

The captain looked down his nose at both of them, then peered around the town. For the moment there was total silence as every man waited for a sight of the enemy.

'Don't look like you scared them too much with your little escapade earlier,' the captain observed.

'I said they'd be back,' Liberty said.

'Fall in with the other men,' the captain barked. 'The redskins are playing with us again and it's about time we taught them a lesson.'

For a moment it looked as though the Englishman was going to make an ill-advised comment, but whatever words he had been about to say remained unspoken when the soldier in the middle of the street suddenly screamed and fell backwards, a flaming arrow lodged in his stomach.

Liberty went down as low as he could and quickly scanned the walls but there was no sign of any Indians. Yet the shot must have come from somewhere up there. At least one Indian had scaled the walls and was hidden up there, amongst the shadows, skilfully moving about unseen by the town's defenders. Once again the walls had been breached.

Suddenly the sky seemed to open up with a brilliant celestial display as flaming arrow upon arrow poured out of the darkness and into the town. As the arrows passed overhead they briefly illuminated the walls and Liberty noticed an Indian crouched not six feet from a soldier. He quickly fired; the Indian toppled forward and fell, already dead, on to the hard ground.

Bedlam followed: soldiers and civilians firing wildly with no clear targets. The flash of rifles competed with the brilliance of the arrows, which continued to come, shot from concealment but devastatingly effective.

More fires broke out. Liberty noticed that the jail-house roof had caught and was now a roaring inferno. The glass in the windows cracked with the heat as the flames spread downwards into the building.

The old man was in there.

Liberty ran towards the jailhouse and came up hard against the front door with his shoulder. He noticed that the Englishman was coming behind him but he had no time to ponder on that. He flung himself through the door and came down heavily on the floor. He groaned and immediately got to his feet, having to cover his face with his bandanna because ot the smoke.

'Get me out of here,' the old man screamed. 'I can't hardly breathe.'

Liberty coughed and wiped his streaming eyes. He could hear the old man but couldn't see anything as he felt his way through a thick cloud of smoke. He made his way from memory, recalling the basic layout of the jailhouse; soon he stood in front of the cell holding the old man.

'Let me out of here,' the old man screamed, holding the bars and frantically yanking them as if his aged muscles had a chance of tearing them from their fittings. 'Hurry up.'

Liberty coughed and wiped his mouth on the back of his hand. A section of the roof gave way and flaming timbers fell around them.

'I don't think I will,' Liberty said, holding the keys up so that the old man could see them.

'What?'

'Let you out of there. Why, you'd only skip town again.'

'Why should you care?' the old man asked. 'Now, come on. Quit stalling.'

'What are you hiding, old man?'

'Open this cell,' the old man yelled. Suddenly another section of the roof caved in and a large plank hit the floor only inches from his feet. Sparks spluttered into the air and a flame immediately caught the old man's bed.

'What are you hiding?' Liberty asked again.

'God-darn it, son! You'd let me burn?'

The bed had now been consumed by the flames, which were now licking greedily at the walls. The atmosphere became oppressive as a treacle-like black fog replaced what little clean air remained.

'Maybe,' Liberty said. 'Now what are you hiding?'

The old man shook his head and stared at Liberty for a moment. 'You'd let me burn?' he repeated; then he obviously decided that Liberty would indeed do that.

'Gold!' he yelled. 'Confederate gold.'

'Best let him out.' Sinclair came up behind Liberty and coughed. 'The air's getting rather hot in here.'

Liberty didn't even bother looking behind him, he just ignored the Englishman. He made as though to open the cell door, but the bars were hot to the touch. For one awful moment the lock refused to budge, the inner workings having been warped by the heat. Then, with a screech of twisting metal the mechanism gave and the door swung open.

'Come on, old-timer.' Liberty grabbed the old man and quickly led him out into the cool night air. They both fell to their knees and coughed until fluid came from their tortured lungs.

'Guess we've got to figure out a way out of here.' Sinclair came up behind them and smiled. 'How much Confederate gold are we talking about?'

'A crateful,' the old man said.

'A crateful split three ways,' Sinclair amended. 'Is it a large crate?'

'Three ways?' The old man was on his feet and bouncing about like a jackrabbit; clearly his recent ordeal had been forgotten now that the question of splitting the gold had been raised. 'It's my gold. I found it and I'm not letting any of you thieving varmints get your hands on it.'

The Englishman smiled and looked at Liberty but the Southerner remained expressionless; he seemed content to sit in the dirt, looking at the chaos around them.

'You need us, old man,' he said after some moments.

'How do you figure that?' the old man asked. 'I never needed nobody no time in my life. And I sure as hell don't need anyone now.'

'You'll never get out of this town without us,' Sinclair told him.

'There's no denying that,' Liberty said. He got to his feet and ran the back of his hand over his mouth. 'English has got a point.'

'And it's stolen gold,' Sinclair continued. 'If I was to inform the army of what you've just said, as some would say is my duty, then they'd find it. You'd end up with nothing. A third is a lot more than nothing at all.'

'Three ways?' The old man looked first at Liberty and then at the Englishman. Around them the chaos continued as the last of the fires were put out. The town had taken a battering since he'd last seen it and when he looked back to the jailhouse he saw the last of the roof fall in, sending sparks into the ochre sky.

'Three ways,' Liberty said. Despite himself, he liked the Englishman's jib.

The old man shrugged his shoulders. A crateful of gold was a lot, maybe too much for one man. At his age a third would keep him in luxury for the remainder of his days.

'Three ways?' He nodded. 'Sure.'

The three men shook hands to seal the deal, then fell silent when they noticed Captain Roberts coming towards them. He had a look like thunder on his face, his eyes blazing as he stared at the old man.

'Who released that man?' he demanded.

'Take a look,' Liberty said. 'There ain't no jail-house no more.'

'Would you have preferred it if we'd let the old-timer burn inside his cell?' Sinclair asked.

'Maybe you should have done just that,' the captain said. 'I don't have the men or the inclination to keep that old man safe.'

'I don't need no safe keeping,' the old-timer retorted.

The captain grabbed the old man and pulled him towards him. He looked straight into his eyes and spoke through lips that were pulled into a feral snarl.

'You try and escape once more,' he warned, 'and I'll order you be shot dead.' With that he pushed the old man backwards, causing him to come down painfully on his rump.

'When I was a younger man I could have whipped you,' the old man said defiantly. 'Reckon I could still whip you.'

'I'm warning you, old man,' the captain snarled,

then he turned on his heel and walked away to the town walls. There he immediately gave the order for all of the men to fall in.

'Well,' Sinclair said presently, 'I suggest we join the fight.'

'It ain't my fight,' the old man said. 'I'm going to my gold.'

'Not yet you ain't,' Liberty told him. He helped the old man to his feet. 'We can't get out of this town until all this is over. If we try and leave the captain will have us shot and even if we did manage to get out we'd still have an Indian army to contend with.'

'Indians don't scare me none,' the old man said.

'Perhaps they should,' said Sinclair. 'Come on, let's get you a rifle. The sooner this is all over the sooner you can take us to that gold.'

CHAPTER THIRTEEN

'The army was here when I got here,' the old man said as they chewed on porridge. 'They'd got here a month or so before I did, that's what I was told. They were still constructing the walls when I came tearing in with half the Indian nation on my tail. They were using the fresh lumber that had been intended for the building of this town.'

Liberty nodded. He too had come into the town with the Indians in hot pursuit. That was only days ago, yet it seemed like another lifetime. He had drifted into the area with no clear notion of where he was going, except away from the madness that had been the civil war. Now he had found another war to occupy him.

'Let's talk about the gold,' Sinclair said, trying to bring the conversation round to the matter at hand.

They had positioned themselves away from the

main centre of activity and sat, nursing their rationed meals, beneath a large tree. Around them soldiers and civilians were running in all directions. Over by the new chuck wagon several other people were eating their breakfasts. Given the amount of activity going on the town was strangely quiet.

The old man's face creased up and he chased a glob of thick porridge around his toothless mouth with his tongue.

'Confederate gold,' he said, then added proudly: 'I hid it myself.'

Liberty and the Englishman exchanged looks but said nothing.

'It'd be safer for you to tell it all,' Sinclair said.

'Is that a threat?' the old man asked, pointing his spoon at the Englishman as if it were a weapon.

'Not at all,' Sinclair replied, mock horror upon his face. 'It's just that with the bloodthirsty savages out there and the army in here there seem to be quite a few obstacles between you and this fabled gold. Now if we – that is my cowboy friend here' – he tapped Liberty on the shoulder – 'and myself knew for certain about this gold, knew that it's not all something you've dreamt up – well you'd have two bodyguards who would fight to the death for you. It's not that we have any warm feelings for you but we have to protect our investment.'

'And then forsake me when you've got my gold?'

'Only a third each, old man.'

'Yeah,' Liberty nodded. 'A third.'

Again the old man's face creased like a dried prune while he tried to work out the arithmetic but then, deciding that it still meant he'd have a fair bit, he nodded.

'So tell us how you came about it, old-timer,' Liberty prompted.

'And where it is? Mustn't forget that,' Sinclair said.

'You men ever heard of the Maxwell brothers?'

'Sure,' Liberty nodded.

The brothers had a reputation across the West. They were known to be deadly and aggressive outlaws. They were powerful men but uncommonly short of stature: Ed, the elder brother, was five feet three inches, while Lon was even an inch or two shorter, but anyone who had the nerve to josh them about their diminutive stature was warned that dynamite comes in small packages; then, as likely as not, the joker was gunned down.

'Ain't heard much about them since before the war,' Liberty added.

'You're not likely to,' the old man said. He lit a quirly he'd rolled from the Englishman's makings. 'They're dead.'

'Could you please get to the point?' Sinclair urged. He snatched his tobacco pouch up from the ground where the old man had dropped it.

'A couple of years ago' – the old man started, then he drew hard on his smoke. He took the smoke deep into his lungs. 'I was—' He went on to tell them how the Maxwell brothers had hit a Confederate bank in Virginia. It had been a massive haul, one of the biggest bank raids on record, and the brothers had fled across the territory with the army in pursuit. They had gone straight across the territory and into Texas, with frequent gunfights between themselves and their pursuers taking place, but the army were soon called off in order to fight the war. The brothers had hidden out in Texas for a spell before fleeing across the border to New Mexico.

It was there that the old man had met up with them.

Of course he recognized them as soon as he saw them, even if the thick sheen of trail dust upon them made them look like penniless hoboes. He had known them as boys back in Iowa, watched them grow from two scruffy kids to a pair of hell-hounds. They too recognized the old man; they knew that he would never cross them so they decided to stick it out and wait for the dust to settle. They figured that given the way the war was going the gold would soon be forgotten. They told the old man to take the gold, hide it somewhere in Arizona territory and then return to New Mexico, where they would be waiting.

He did as he had been told; he'd taken the gold across much of Arizona and then buried it where he knew he'd be able to retrieve it when the time was right. The Maxwells promised him a goodly share when the danger was over. Not for one moment had he thought about taking all the gold and vanishing because he knew the brothers would hunt him down and kill him slowly, making him suffer for his betrayal. They'd do worse than kill him outright: they would only finish him off when he pleaded for an end to the suffering.

'They was a pair of sadistic sons of bitches,' the old man concluded.

'So what happened to these hellhounds?' Sinclair asked. The old man frowned.

'I'm getting there,' he said. 'I was gone maybe a month or six weeks and when I returned I learned the brothers were dead, shot down by the Union army after being caught in the crossfire of a battle.'

'How very convenient,' Sinclair said. 'The money became yours by default.'

The old man looked at the Englishman and nodded.

'As soon as news got out that the Maxwells were dead a Confederate troop turned up, looking for the gold. So I decided to stay put for a while and then get the gold when the time was right.'

'You waited a long time?' Liberty said, working a knot out of his neck with one hand. The old man nodded.

'I waited till the war ended and then some. When I finally went out to get my reward the army set upon me. They were amazed the marauding savages hadn't scalped me, so they brought me here. Mind you, I had a few dozen Apaches on my tail when they came across me so I was kinda grateful.' He spat on to the ground.

'And you're still here,' Liberty said.

'I'm still here,' the old man agreed, glumly.

'And you know exactly where the gold is?' Sinclair asked. The old man nodded and pointed to his head.

'I've a map in here.'

'Then until this is over,' English said, 'you've got two guardian angels.'

'Oh yeah,' Liberty said. 'You're carrying a mighty valuable document in your head.'

CHAPTER
FOURTEEN

The Indians were back.

Liberty stood beside the captain on the upper ledge of the front wall. The Englishman was down on the street, keeping the old man tucked away so that there was no chance of a stray arrow coming flying through the sky and ruining their chances of ever getting their hands on the gold. He was, Sinclair had said, protecting their interests.

So far the Indians had made no move to attack. Maybe fifty braves sat there upon their mounts, watching the town. Less than ten minutes ago the bugle had sounded, warning of the Indians' arrival, but so far they had made no move to approach the town. They were keeping well back, wary of the incredible range demonstrated by the gun during the previous night's raid.

'What's happening?' Captain Roberts asked of no one in particular. Troopers were lined up along the ledge, their rifles aimed at the Indians, though so far no one had fired. The Indians were out of rifle range in any case.

'They want to talk,' Liberty said. 'They're sitting there inviting us to parley.'

'They're savages.' Roberts spat the words out with contempt. 'You can't converse with a savage. You certainly can't trust them and I'm not going to send a man out there to be brutalized.'

Five braves moved forward of the main force, approaching the town, then they came to a halt. In the lead, mounted on a magnificent white mustang, was the chief. His splendid lance was decorated with eagle feathers that fluttered in the gentle breeze. The chief sat on his horse, head back, regarding the town down his long aquiline nose. He certainly looked impressive.

'Let me go out and talk to them,' Liberty said. 'I've dealt with Indians before; I can speak their language and it can't hurt to hear them out.'

'They may kill you.'

'I'm prepared to take that risk,' Liberty said.

The captain looked at him with suspicion and then at the ragtag bunch of survivors left in the town. The Indians certainly had the upper hand, both in strength of numbers and confidence. They had thousands of braves in the hills, yet only a few had come here today as a delegation, which betokened a level of self-assurance that almost equated to arrogance. They all wore war paint and carried bows as well as rifles, but so far they hadn't made any threatening moves.

'Why should I trust a Reb?' the captain said presently.

'What would I do?' Liberty asked. 'Run away? Join up with the Indians and attack the town? Seems to me you've got nothing to lose by letting me go out there and everything to gain. At least we'll find out what the Indians' intentions are.'

The captain considered things for a moment, then nodded.

'But tell those savages they are dealing with the United States army and we will subdue them.'

'Sure,' Liberty said.

He waved his arms about in full view of the Indians, signalling that he was coming out to talk. He went to the nearest ladder and climbed down into the street, then the captain gave the orders for him to be allowed out, adding that the town gates were to be closed and locked behind him.

Liberty smiled as he heard that. Then, after giving the Englishman a stern look, he stepped out of the town and into the Indian-occupied territory beyond.

He stood there while the gates were shut behind him and the large lock slid into place. Slowly he reached down and unbuckled his gunbelt, then held it above his head in full view of the Indians. He allowed it to drop to the ground and then stepped over it.

He took a last look back at the town. He noticed the captain looking down at him from the ledge and he smiled wryly. He hoped none of the soldiers would develop an itch in their trigger fingers and fire at the waiting Indians.

That would be apt to get him killed.

'I come to talk,' he yelled. 'I am unarmed.'

Liberty started the long walk towards the Indians.

The Indians remained impassive, watching the lone white man walk towards them. Their leader, Chayton, regarded him with eyes that were squinted to narrow slits against the hot desert sun. He had courage: that much was plainly evident to the Indian chief. It was a quality he admired but seldom saw in white men.

Liberty stopped a few feet from the Indians. He looked directly into the face of their chief and put a hand to his chest.

'Liberty,' he said.

The Indians obviously understood him: at least

the chief seemed to, but the mounted braves remained staring at him impassively, their eyes void of any emotion. There was no real hate there: they seemed simply to regard him as of no significance to them.

'Chayton,' the chief said, presently, tapping his own chest. His horse snorted as if to endorse the name. 'I speak your tongue.'

'Like a native,' Liberty said with a grin.

'You are the white chief?' Chayton regarded him for a moment. The white man seemed strangely familiar to him but that he was the chief seemed impossible.

'No,' Liberty said. 'I speak for the white chief. I come to you to talk and carry your words back to the white chief.'

The chief stared at Liberty with an intensity that the white man found uncomfortable. The Indian's eyes seemed to bore deep into his soul.

Liberty felt uneasy. He had in the past had dealings with Sioux, Comanches and the Blackfeet, but never Apaches. All five of the Indians were clearly of the Apache nation and, with the exception of the chief, they were now looking down at him with contempt.

'Tell your people to go from this place,' Chayton said. 'They will not be harmed if they leave today. If they still remain after the sun sets and again rises,

119

then they will be killed. All of them. None will be spared.'

'They will not leave,' Liberty said.

'Then they choose death. It is a simple choice.' Chayton spoke the words in a matter-of-fact tone. This was no idle threat.

'Soon more white men will come,' Liberty said. He stood perfectly erect, not wanting to show any fear to the Indians; he looked like granite but in truth he was absolutely terrified and his heart seemed to have jumped into the back of his throat.

'Then we will kill them also.'

'No.' Liberty shook his head. 'I do not believe that is true. They have guns that can kill many in the blink of an eye, cannons that can destroy your villages.'

The chief raised his lance up above his head and let out a blood-chilling scream. For one awful moment Liberty thought the chief was going to throw the weapon, killing him outright. The Indian did not attack, though; he lowered his lance and smiled at the white man, who had still not flinched.

'You have much courage. Your words carry steel,' he said. 'I will respect that and allow you to return to your people. We shall return to ours.'

Liberty nodded, said nothing.

'When we return,' the chief continued, 'then you shall die, along with the rest of your people.'

The Indians turned their mounts but Liberty stopped them.

'Wait,' he said. The Indian chief turned once more to face him.

'Speak.' Chayton looked at him with impatience.

'We have women and children in the town,' Liberty said, looking the chief firmly in the eye. 'Allow them to leave with civilian men as their guides.'

Chayton seemed to consider the proposal for a moment. Then he gave his answer.

'Two men shall be allowed to leave with the women and children. The men can carry one rifle each but no other weapons. They are to go north and keep on going.'

'They will pass in peace?'

'You have my word they will not be assaulted in any way,' Chayton said. Then he pointed an admonitory finger at Liberty. 'But any tricks and they will be slaughtered, be it man, woman or child. Their blood will be on your hands then.'

'There will be no tricks,' Liberty promised.

'Then they will be allowed to go on their way.' The chief raised a hand to swat at a fly that was worrying his horse.

'You are a man of honour,' Liberty said. 'I take your word as the truth.'

At that the Indians rode off, leaving Liberty

standing in what had quickly become a no man's land. He watched them disappear over the distant ridge, then he turned and walked back to Red Rock. The sun, impossibly bright in the sky, beat down with relentless mercy but the day seemed to have a hint of darkness about it.

CHAPTER FIFTEEN

A town meeting was called.

The Indian delegation had left. Outside the town the landscape seemed deserted and eerily quiet. The sun beat down from a clear sky and the parched land shimmered beneath its harsh power. The indigenous animal life had adapted to the environment and everything from the smallest insect to the largest mammal sought shelter from the life-sapping heat. An ocean of sun-parched dust stretched out to the far horizon, everything looking as motionless as if in a painting.

The captain held court. He stood outside the ruins of the saloon, where everyone in the town had gathered. Liberty had just finished speaking, telling the entire town of the offer the Indians had made. The final decision as to whether the women and children would leave was down to the captain.

It had surprised Liberty that he had been allowed to share the details of his meeting with the Indians; he had been sure the captain would keep the information from the townsfolk: that it would be for the captain alone to make the decision on the Indian chief's offer. But the captain seemed to have changed; he was not as full of bluster as he had been previously. Maybe it was the endless wait for the expected reinforcements to arrive that was troubling him; whatever the reason, he was going to temporarily relax his own authority and allow the townspeople to decide whether anyone should leave.

'How long before reinforcements get here?' someone shouted out from the back of the expectant crowd.

'Maybe tomorrow or the day after,' the captain answered bluntly. 'They are coming as quickly as they can. The army is fully stretched and is having to police over two and a half million square miles from the Missouri to the Eastern Sierras because of marauding savages.'

'Can we hold out for more than a day?' Sinclair asked.

The captain looked at Liberty, then nodded.

A murmur passed around the crowd, then a man stepped forward and stood before the captain.

'I will stay and fight,' the man said. 'But I would

be happier if my wife and children were taken to safety. I'm sure most men feel the same way.'

A cheer erupted from the crowd indicating that this was indeed the general feeling. They had all been beaten down this last week or so and the women looked haggard; the children too were at the end of their tether and would snap with maybe one more attack. It made sense for them to leave. Men could fight better when they didn't have to keep one eye trained on their respective wives and children. When it came down to the grim and gritty reality of battle it was quite often every man for himself.

'Can we trust these savages?' a spindly-looking man towards the front of the crowd asked. All eyes, the captain's included, turned on Liberty. He seemed to have become the official spokesman where the Indians were concerned.

'I think so,' he said. 'They just want us off this land.'

'I don't in the least care what the savages want,' the captain said. 'Their wishes are not my concern. It is my duty to protect this town and the land upon which it stands.'

'The women and children shall leave,' a short, squat man said, pushing himself to the front of the crowd. 'That seems the sensible move to make.'

*

125

'Listen to me,' Sinclair said. 'A full half-share is much more than a third.'

The old man looked at the Englishman.

'I don't know what to say. That's mighty devious.'

Moments ago, while everyone was occupied with the town meeting, the Englishman had spirited the old man behind the ruins of the livery stables. Here they were both out of sight and earshot of anyone else.

'This is as good a chance to get out of here as we're going to get,' Sinclair said.

'Leave all these folk to face the Indians alone?'

'It's not our fight.' The Englishman smiled. 'Besides, you never showed much concern for the townsfolk during your escape attempts.'

The old man scratched his chin. 'I don't know.'

'I leave it to you,' Sinclair said. 'I mean, we can either stay and fight – and most likely perish at the hands of the vastly superior Indian numbers, or we can spirit ourselves away when the wagon leaves with the women and children. We can be enjoying our wealth while these fools fight a losing battle.'

'Don't seem fair somehow,' the old man demurred.

'I repeat,' the Englishman said, 'that didn't seem to bother you the last time you legged it.'

'Things have changed,' the old man replied.

'Look.' Sinclair grabbed the old man forcefully

by the arm. 'There's going to be a wagon leaving here shortly and somewhere out there that gold is waiting for us. You could live like a king for the rest of your life. If we stay and fight then the chances are that we may never see it.'

'It's my gold,' the old man said. 'I'm entitled to it.'

'Agreed. But if we stay here the Indians will probably overrun the place and we'll all lose our scalps. The gold will serve no purpose to a corpse. You can't spend the money when you're dead, old man.'

'How will we get out without being seen?'

'Leave that to me.' The Englishman looked around them. 'Come on,' he said. 'Let's get back before we're missed.'

CHAPTER SIXTEEN

'Get those people moving,' the captain yelled. 'Before I change my mind.'

The townsmen stood in the middle of the street and watched as their respective wives, children and friends clambered on to the two wagons. There were over forty of them, including the two men who had been elected to drive the wagons. There had been tearful farewells, hugs, kisses and handshakes, wishes of good luck, and now it was time to leave the beleaguered town.

The wagons were driven forward. A pair of troopers had started to remove the locking mechanism from the gates when the bugle sounded.

The Indians were back.

'Hold your fire!' the captain yelled. Liberty gave him a look as if to say: *You're learning.*

Both men ran towards the ladders and climbed up to the ledge.

The Englishman, standing next to the old man, watched Liberty and the captain climb the ladders. Then he nudged the old man.

'Now's our chance,' he said. 'Now remember what I told you.'

The old man nodded, eager to go.

'Hold on with all your might. The straps will help but don't let go until you hear me yelling.'

The old man nodded again.

'Don't worry about me,' he said. 'I've been in fixes a heck of a lot worse than this one.'

'I bet you have,' Sinclair said and rolled his eyes. He would have to keep a tight rein on the old-timer who, decrepit or not, could still be a great deal of trouble.

Earlier, while the details of the wagons' departure were being worked out the Englishman had stolen several leather straps from the livery stable. He had been careful not to be spotted while he slid beneath the two wagons – the only ones in town still in workable condition – and tied the straps to the central support so that they created a harness of sorts that could hold a man, unseen beneath the wagon.

The wagons, like all those intended for use on the frontier, had been built high and strong in order to negotiate the rough terrain. The Englishman knew they would have to remain beneath the wagons for several rough miles and he was confident the straps would support them.

Without the straps taking their weight it would be impossible to hold on to the wagon for more than a few hundred yards. The old man would probably not be capable of even that distance.

'Ready then?' Sinclair said.

The old man nodded.

'Then come on.' The Englishman led the way, dragging the old man behind him.

They both ran to the wagons; then, after taking a furtive look around, the Englishman slid beneath one of the wagons and the old man did likewise under the other.

They each slipped the straps over their wrists and feet and hung there, suspended a foot or so above the ground, invisible to anyone watching the wagons going by.

Now we wait, Sinclair thought. Which was always the most difficult part.

'They are not here for war,' Liberty said, turning to the captain, who was leaning against the ledge looking at the Indians who had gathered outside. 'Not this time. They are only here to observe as our people leave. You can't blame them for that.'

'I hope you're right.' The captain scratched his chin and spat over the edge of the wall. He didn't suppose he had any choice other than to allow the wagons to leave and hope for the best. The Reb seemed convinced that the Indians would allow the women and children safe passage and, despite his initial animosity towards the man, he was starting to trust him. The fact that Liberty had saved his life earlier was obviously part of the reason for his change of heart.

'They're not a war party,' Liberty pointed out. 'It's the same group as earlier. They're just here to watch our people go.'

'How can you be so sure?'

'Simple,' Liberty said. 'We have their word. It's the honourable thing to do.'

'The "noble savage",' the captain said. 'Still don't trust the bastards, though.'

The captain gave the signal for the gates to be opened and he stood there watching the wagons leave. The men up on the ledge held their weapons at the ready in case the Indians attacked but until the Indians made the first move they were under strict orders to maintain the cease fire.

The wagons headed north. The Indians showed no inclination to pursue them, only paying them perfunctory interest as they vanished into the distance. Then the chief galloped forward, the other braves remaining where they were.

'Hold your fire,' Liberty said. 'He's coming alone. Let this play out.'

The troopers on either side of Liberty looked at the captain for confirmation. He nodded his head and, though the men remained tense, they lowered their rifles slightly.

Liberty watched as the Indian chief drew his horse up alongside the town wall and looked up at them.

'Your women and young ones have left?' the chief asked.

'They have,' Liberty said. The chief didn't seem to have much idea of military protocol: he was addressing him directly, seeming to ignore the men in uniform. The Indian would know that he presented an easy target to the white men but he had no fear. He had trusted the word of the one called Liberty.

'Then we will return with the sun,' Chayton said. 'Those of you that remain here then will die.'

'I could kill him now,' the captain whispered out of the side of his mouth. 'Deliver that bad medicine now.'

'No,' Liberty murmured, 'that'll bring the entire lot down on us and probably get the women and children killed in retaliation. By dawn the wagons will be long gone.'

The captain looked at Liberty and grinned.

'You seem to have taken command, Reb. I think you need to remember who is in charge here, who gives the orders.'

Liberty shrugged and turned back to face Chayton. He stood proudly looking the Indian straight in the eye, careful to show no fear.

'We will give you a good battle,' he said.

Chayton nodded and a brittle smile crossed his features. He pulled his horse under control and looked back, his gaze directed at Liberty, ignoring everyone else. He raised his lance and extended his chest, pulling his head back as he spoke.

'You will die well,' he said, and turned his horse with the skill of a man who had spent his life on horseback. He rode back to his people. When he reached them they fell in behind him and soon they were all galloping away.

'What do you suggest we do now?'

Liberty wasn't sure whether the captain was being sarcastic or not, but he answered none the less:

'Take a full inventory of our weapons and ammunition,' he said. 'We need to get ready for a fight to end all fights.'

'Savages!' The captain spat out the word as he watched the Indian party vanish into the distance.

'And then get some sleep,' Liberty said. 'Real

sleep because we need to be ready. Tomorrow this is all going to end one way or another.'

'Don't you think the Indians will try and surprise us? Come tonight when our guard is down?'

'No.' Liberty looked out at the glimmering desert. The wagons too had disappeared over the far horizon. A few scattered clouds had formed in the darkening sky. The dying sun highlighted the large rocks that scattered the desert, bringing out their natural coppery colour beneath the reddening sky.

'Honour matters more than victory to the Indians.' Liberty said presently. 'It would be a hollow victory without honour. They have said dawn and that's when they'll come. Not before.'

'You place great credence in the words of a savage,' the captain said. He'd never really encountered many Indians, but he'd learnt plenty about them back at West Point. They were savages and their minds were not given to cold reason. They acted on a primitive level and although many were placid and peaceful none of them were to be trusted.

' "Savage" is your term,' Liberty said. 'Not mine.'

'God forgive me, Reb, but I'm gonna trust you. You'd better be right. We've got little chance when we are prepared for them, but taken by surprise we'd be beaten hollow.'

'They won't come till dawn,' Liberty repeated.

'We must hold them off,' the captain said. 'The reinforcements can't be too many days away. If we can hold them off till then. . . .'

'We can try,' Liberty said. 'We can try.'

'Every man left within these walls will have to fight like two men,' the captain said.

'Then we'd better prepare.'

Liberty knew they had little chance. When the Indians next attacked it would be with a stronger force than ever, and they would keep coming, no matter how many braves fell, until they had breached the walls. Once that was done they would slaughter every man remaining.

The captain nodded and gave the order for everyone to gather in the street, sentries included.

The Indians weren't going to attack till dawn.

They had given their word.

CHAPTER SEVENTEEN

Night brought an uneasy peace to Red Rock.

Liberty sat outside the jailhouse and stared off into the night. He was fuming over the Englishman and the old-timer; he knew he'd been a fool to trust the Englishman to keep the old-timer in check. He had been so focused on getting the women and children to safety that he had dropped his guard, and allowed Sinclair and the old man to spirit themselves away with the wagons that had left the town.

He'd been careless, he'd been stupid – and wasn't that the truth! It had taken Liberty a good hour or so after the wagons had gone before he'd noticed the sons of bitches' absence. Things had been hectic though, so he at least had a reason for his mistake, but all the same he felt as a dumb as a rock for trusting the English lord.

Shortly after the wagons had left all those remaining in the town had gathered in the street and a full inventory of weapons and ammunition was made. Tactics for the coming battle were discussed and everyone was told to enjoy double helpings from the chuck wagon. Whiskey would be available but each man would be limited to three glasses to ensure a clear head come morning. It was only then that Liberty noticed the absence of both the Englishman and the old-timer.

Liberty shook his head and closed his eyes.

He had better things to think of at the moment but the Englishman wouldn't stay far from his mind. If he ever saw the cowardly double-crossing son of a bitch again he'd kill him. If Sinclair did manage to get away and uncover the gold he hoped it would bring a curse on him. Sure, a crate of Confederate gold, likely missing and forgotten since the war, was quite an enticement, but running out on the townspeople, leaving them to fight against the massive Indian horde was more than cowardly. It was downright evil.

Soon Liberty fell into a light sleep and although he rested he was aware of every minute ticking away towards dawn.

*

137

'Damn and blast!' said Sinclair, then he smiled apologetically. 'I'm afraid spending so much time on the frontier has coloured my language some- what.'

The old man looked at him with a blank expres- sion. He spat tobacco juice on to the ground. 'Wish you'd talk good old American.'

'You'd swear you'd invented the language,' the Englishman replied. He peered into the darkness, trying to get their bearings. 'The only thing I know for sure is we're nowhere near London.'

'Follow me,' the old man said. He led Sinclair across a tumble of rocks and towards a large hill. 'I knows where I'm going.'

The two men had remained suspended beneath their respective wagons for at least two miles. Once they had let go of their supporting straps and fallen to the ground they had quickly scrambled for cover and remained there for maybe thirty minutes while the wagons rolled on and out of sight. No one on the wagons had known they were there, suspended beneath them, and the pair had made the journey without discovery. The Indian party had followed the wagons for a short distance but as soon as the procession had gone a mile or so out of town the Indians had turned their mounts and headed back to their own people.

The Englishman smiled at how easy his escape

from the town had been, took pride in the ease with which he had managed to spirit the old man away, fooling that dumb American. He felt himself to be very much a wily old fox.

Now night had fallen quickly and the English lord felt on edge as he followed the old man across the rugged landscape. They made slow progress over the rock-strewn ground and with each step they seemed to be moving perilously closer to the Indian encampment. His feet throbbed and he cursed his choice of footwear, whilst suited to the saloon his shoes were most definitely not holding up to the trudge around the wilderness.

'I hope you know where you're going,' Sinclair said, speaking in little more than a whisper. It was difficult keeping upright while walking over such rocky ground. He was looking forward to hitting the open desert again. Struggling through the dusty sands would surely be easier than this.

The old man looked at the Englishman and shook his head.

'I know this land as well as I know the back of my own hand,' he said. 'I could walk around with my eyes closed and I'd still know where I was.'

'Oh good.' Sinclair smiled. 'Then we're perfectly safe.'

The sarcasm was lost on the old man, who sniffed, spat and farted before moving off again.

The fart had been loud, and potent in the olfactory department. If the Indians hadn't heard it then there was a very good chance that they would smell it.

'You have some truly endearing qualities,' Sinclair said, keeping his head down as he trudged along behind the old man.

'Half the time,' the old man complained, 'I don't know what you're talking about.'

'Just as well,' Sinclair said. 'Just as well.'

They continued onwards for some distance, only stopping to rest when they reached a hilly area. Now they were dangerously close to the Indian encampment and the old man told the Englishman so. He also informed him that nevertheless they had to pass close to where the Indians were encamped in order to get to the place where the gold was hidden.

'Maybe we should find somewhere to hide out?' Sinclair suggested. 'Wait until the Indians move out to attack the town before we go on.'

'No.' The old man shook his head. 'It won't be all of the redskins who go on the warpath. Those that remain will spot us easily come daylight. Our only chance is to pass by them during the night.'

'Do you think we could do that?' Sinclair asked.

The old man shrugged his shoulders.

'Got any tobaccy?' he asked.

'No,' said Sinclair. He reached into his breast pocket and pulled out two of the long thin cigars he favoured. 'I've got these, though.'

The old man smiled, revealing chipped and dirty teeth. He took one of the cigars.

'Obliged,' he said and searched through his oversized trousers for a match. 'Damn!'

Sinclair took a lucifer from his pocket, struck it against a rock, lit his own cigar and held the flame out to the old man.

'That's good,' the old man said, blowing a thick cloud of fragrant blue-grey smoke into the night air.

'We can't stay here,' said Sinclair, peering into the darkness but seeing nothing other than shadows.

'Just long enough to finish this here smoke,' the old man said and again drew hard on the cigar.

Somewhere in the distance the hoot of an owl mingled in with other night sounds and the Englishman felt a shiver run down his spine.

CHAPTER EIGHTEEN

Dawn arrived.

Red Rock instantly came alive, exploding into activity as men took up their positions. Arms and ammunition were placed at strategic points to allow reloading with little interruption to the actual battle. It was felt that this one would be the big one, that it would all be over one way or another before the reinforcements eventually arrived. Today would be the day of reckoning, with the Indians throwing everything they had at the town's defenders. They would be confident, as the depleted force within the town would be no match for a large Indian force.

'The Indians won't really gather tightly,' Liberty said. 'They'll scatter and come from all sides, but I want to be ready with that dynamite as soon as I get my best chance. Someone will have to be standing by ready to light it at my command.'

The captain nodded. 'You think that idea will work?'

'I guess so. Reckon I can get it way out there.'

The evening before Liberty had cut up a piece of hide and made it into small loops with which to sling rocks over the town walls. He had pulled the hide loops tightly round the rocks, swung the long end around a few times and then hurled it away, making the rocks travel great distances. He'd learned to do this as a kid and had grown so skilled that he had brought down a few rabbits and often larger game with the blunt projectiles.

He had the dynamite; both sticks attached to a length of strong string. They too were tied tightly to a loop, together with a stone to give weight. He had capped each stick with a medium-length fuse. The only problem was that the fuse was apt to go out during its journey through the air, but he had bound it thickly to increase its chances of staying alight.

Buckets of water had been brought into the middle of the street and left there in case they were needed to fight any fires. Water buckets had also been placed at strategic places along the ledges at the top of the town walls. Animal grease had been poured over the walls to make it impossible for the Indians to climb up, taking advantage of weakly defended areas, during the battle.

The soldiers and civilians of Red Rock were as ready as they would ever be.

'No sign of them yet,' Captain Roberts said.

Liberty gazed into the heat haze of a day that was already starting to get very hot.

'They'll be here,' he said.

'I hope they hurry up.' It was clear from the twitch the captain had developed that he was finding the tension of the wait more draining than the thought of the battle itself. He wasn't the only one. There was not a man in the town who was not ready to snap at any moment.

Liberty thought for a moment of the English lord, but quickly put him from his mind. He wondered if he was still out there in the wilderness looking for the old man's gold, or maybe he was on his way to Tucson, the gold already retrieved.

'Damn you!' Liberty said, mumbling to himself. It was likely, given the odds they were now facing, that he would never see the Englishman again, would never be able to get him to answer for his treachery.

The bugle sounded as the first wave of Indians was spotted in the far distance. Every man in the town sprang alert as though with one coordinated movement. Liberty gazed out and stared open-mouthed as he saw hundreds upon hundreds of tiny figures coming over the skyline. They were galloping towards the town and became an angry swarm lost in the dust cloud as they approached.

'Hold your fire,' Liberty said. 'Wait until they're close enough.'

The captain slapped Liberty on the shoulder and nodded.

'Do as he says,' he ordered his men.

'Now the real thing starts,' Liberty muttered.

'I may have misjudged you,' the captain said with a laugh. 'You're a wily Reb, sure enough.'

'And you ain't so bad for a yellow leg,' Liberty replied with a wry smile. Then his attention was diverted as the advancing Indians stopped and another wave of even greater numbers appeared on the horizon and started advancing. There seemed to be thousands of the Indians out there.

The second wave came forward but much more slowly and eventually there appeared to be two men being forced along on foot ahead of them.

'Dadblast it!' Liberty said as realization hit him. So English and the old-timer hadn't got very far at all before being captured. He guessed they had been taken captive at some time during the night, which was why the Indians were late in arriving and had missed first light. They obviously had some use for the two white men.

'It's our missing men,' the captain said.

'Yeah.' Liberty nodded; he guessed that right now the English lord would be wishing he'd stayed in town and faced the fight. His chances would have far better within these walls than they were out amongst the enemy.

'Serve them right. Dammed cowards!' The captain had no pity for the two men who had ignored his orders and, as far as he was concerned, had fled from the town with no thought other than that of saving their own skins. Liberty had to admit he agreed with the captain.

'Trouble is the Indians will think we double-crossed them with the wagons. The way they'll see it is that we smuggled those two out with the women and children, hoping they would spy on them or even attack. They'll figure the two men had been intended to assassinate the chiefs in the hope of causing chaos amongst the gathered tribes.'

'Don't make much difference what the damn Indians think,' the captain said. 'It ain't going to change anything that happens here today.'

'Not to us, maybe.' Liberty took the makings from his shirt and got himself a quirly going. He took the smoke deeply into his lungs and felt the nicotine immediately steady his nerves. 'To those two it's going to make all the difference.' He allowed the smoke to escape slowly between his teeth.

146

'I think we're about to find out.' The captain pointed down as both groups of Indians came together and the Englishman and the old man were thrown on to the ground in front of the chief's horse.

'Hold your fire,' he yelled, aware that just about now his men must be feeling as jumpy as bugs on a hot plate.

'God help them! 'Liberty said.

He knew what was coming. In the eyes of the Indians the two men had acted with dishonour. They would die slowly, painfully, without being allowed the dignity of defending themselves in battle. Maybe now would be the time to send the first stick of dynamite out. There were many of the braves gathered close by and he was confident that a stick flung amongst them all would cause maximum carnage. Of course it wouldn't help the Englishman or the old-timer, but then they were beyond help. They had no hope of surviving, no matter which way things went today.

He looked down at the first stick and nodded to the trooper assigned to light it.

'Get ready,' he half-whispered, but hold it until I say.'

Liberty didn't give a second thought for the fortune the old-timer claimed was hidden out there among the hills; if the gold the old man had talked about ever had existed it was gone for ever now.

The captain looked at Liberty and then down at the dynamite. He shook his head, shrugged his shoulders and looked out at the countless Indian braves.

Chayton had stepped from his horse and was standing over the two white men. He jabbed a foot into the Englishman's stomach.

'We allowed your women and young to leave,' he yelled. 'We trusted the white man and once again we are betrayed. These men will die first.'

'Good,' Sinclair shouted defiantly; he was struggling against the bindings on his arms but it was futile. 'I never was one for waiting around. I'd like to get this over with and take afternoon tea in the next world.'

The old-timer said nothing, but as far as Liberty could tell he was sobbing.

'They're going to torture them,' Liberty said. 'I should use the dynamite now but I can't blow those two guys up.'

'They're going to die anyway,' the captain said. 'That much is inevitable and if now is the best chance to use the dynamite, when it will be most effective, then we should take that chance.'

Liberty handed one of the sticks to the captain.

'They'll die,' he said. 'But I can't see them tortured. They'll go cleanly, with a bullet through the head.' He pulled his Colt from leather and spun the chamber. 'When I shoot you throw that stick straight over and then duck. Swing it hard, get it right out there.'

The captain nodded, then looked at the trooper who was waiting with the large sulphur matches.

'Light it on this man's command,' he told the trooper.

Liberty nodded and turned his attention back to the terrible scene below.

'Am I going to get a haircut?' the Englishman quipped as he saw the glint of the blade that Chayton was pushing towards his stomach.

Liberty had to admire English's nerve.

He was not such a coward after all. Still, the Southerner knew that, courageous or not, he would soon start screaming when the blade was pushed into soft flesh, started to cut through muscle and tear the organs beneath. The pain would be intense and the wound fatal, but death would take time to come; life would bleed out of him, each drop burning as it ran from the wound.

It would be far better to die quickly, painlessly.

One sudden blow and then lights out.

'God forgive me,' Liberty said. Then suddenly he stood up and shot.

Liberty's aim was perfect; he saw the hole open up in the centre of the Englishman's forehead. The shot startled Chayton, who dropped the blade and looked up at the man with the gun, but Liberty had no time to notice. He took aim at the old man, who was cowering next to Sinclair's corpse. Again he fired; the old man was thrown backwards by the force of the bullet as it took him squarely in the face.

'Throw that dynamite,' Liberty shouted.

Then the dynamite went over but the captain hadn't thrown it with enough force and it was still close to the wall when it exploded. Liberty couldn't get a shot at the Indian chief before the inevitable explosion.

The world suddenly turned a blinding white and all the air seemed to be sucked out of him, to be replaced by a searing dust that burnt his lungs.

Liberty felt himself thrown backwards from the ledge, falling through the air to the hard ground below.

CHAPTER NINETEEN

Part of the town wall had been blown apart in the explosion. The Indians had broken through into the town and were now fighting in the street. Many men had already died but the battle for Red Rock raged on.

Liberty had been knocked unconscious by the dynamite; he had landed on the chuck wagon, the canvas breaking his fall and wrapping itself around him. Now as he came round he could see the mayhem going on all about him. He didn't have any time to think about the situation or to evaluate his position; he just rolled over, pushing the canvas from him. He came to his feet and immediately grabbed a Colt from the ground; he shot an Indian through the head, then took another brave in the chest.

He ran for some sort of cover and dived down

behind an upturned table.

'Over here, Reb.'

Liberty spun in the direction of the yell and saw the captain and maybe a dozen men: troopers and civilians, firing from the ruins of the saloon. Part of the building was still standing and gave them some protection from the arrows and bullets the Indians were sending their way. They fought on valiantly even though it seemed inevitable that they would eventually fall. Each of them knew this and yet they continued to fight.

The enemy simply had the strength of numbers to ensure that victory was his.

Liberty looked around him and shuddered at the sight that greeted him. The Indians had already won. That much was clear; all that remained was for the rest of the town's defenders to die; there would be no surrender. The buildings that were still standing were on fire, there were bodies strewn everywhere, and as Liberty watched he saw another section of the stockade wall cave in. Soon nothing of the walls would remain and Red Rock would be no more than a smouldering ruin in the middle of the desert.

A brave saw Liberty and ran towards him, screaming at the top of his voice, but he was thrown backwards as Liberty's gun sounded and the bullet took him through the throat, sending a fine spray of blood into the air.

'They're everywhere!' Liberty yelled.

'It's every man for himself!' the captain yelled back. He fired a Winchester at a brave who tore past on horseback. His aim was good and the Indian seemed to be lifted from the horse by unseen hands and then deposited, already dead, on the ground.

Liberty shot another brave and then another, then he was thrown backwards when an arrow entered his left shoulder. He hit the ground hard but came back up and gritted his teeth against the pain. He fired again and then saw the captain's head explode as an Indian bullet tore through his skull. Liberty spotted the Indian who had fired the shot and took him out before he could fire again.

On realizing that Captain Roberts was dead the men in the ruins of the saloon suddenly burst out into the street, where they started screaming and firing their weapons wildly. One by one they were gunned down as the Indians returned fire. Some of them were shot with arrows and Liberty noticed one man take a fierce-looking tomahawk in the face, the axe crushing his head as easily as if it were a large melon. The man stumbled about for several moments, a gruesome sight, before falling down dead.

Liberty saw Chayton positioned where the town gates had once stood. He sat astride his horse, a magnificent pure-white creature, and watched as his braves tasted victory and took what was left of the town apart.

'Bastard!' Liberty growled. He lifted the Colt.

He had one bullet left in the chamber and no time to reload if he missed. His finger tensed on the trigger just as the chief spotted him. Their eyes locked.

Something neither man understood passed between them, but Liberty was sure he saw the chief smile an instant before the Colt's heavy slug blasted away the Indian's face.

Liberty screamed and then fell forward as a bullet winged his leg. He hit the ground and found himself falling into a blackness that was suddenly engulfing him.

It's over, he thought.

Soon there was nothingness.

Liberty came around some time after dark.

At first he thought he was dead and that this place was hell. It certainly felt like it, smelt like it, the air tasted like it: there were bodies everywhere he looked, most of them white, some of them scalped.

A sickly-sharp scent of wood smoke and death hung heavy in the air and the silence only made it all the more terrible.

Liberty examined himself and found he had an arrowhead in his shoulder; the shaft must have fallen off when he collapsed. There was a flesh wound on his left leg, which throbbed like hell but otherwise didn't seem too bad. The arrowhead would have to come out and the wound be cleaned and dressed, but he'd survive.

He pulled himself to his feet and stood there for some time.

From the way he figured it he had taken part in a major battle and was the sole survivor. How the Indians had missed him when they had ransacked the town it was beyond him to comprehend but he supposed it was something for him to be grateful for. He thought about the Englishman, and the old-timer with his stories of hidden gold. He wasn't at all sure if the old man had been telling the truth or not but he guessed he'd never find out now.

Despite the situation he laughed, finding grim humour in the way things had turned out.

He reached into his shirt, took out his makings and rolled himself a smoke. His shoulder smarted with the movement but he ignored it. As he smoked he heard a far-off bugle sound, then came the thundering hoofs of countless horses as they raced through the night towards the smouldering town.

'Here come the reinforcements,' Liberty said. 'Ain't much to reinforce.'

He fell backwards on to his rump.

He started laughing uncontrollably.

He was still laughing when the fourteen-hundred-strong army rode into Red Rock.

EPILOGUE

In 1868 the Fort Laramie Treaty was signed, in which the Black Hills were promised to the Lakota people, but when gold was discovered in the hills and prospectors moved in violence flared up again. That same year the Bozeman forts, designed to keep the Bozeman trail open and to afford protection to the settlers, were abandoned.

Years of battles continued. Then in 1871 Sitting Bear was killed. A year later Cochise surrendered and would die in captivity in 1874. Two years later the ownership of the Black Hills was still a bone of contention and General Custer was sent to subdue the Lakota people who were attacking prospectors and wagon trains. This would culminate in the Battle of the Little Big Horn in which Custer and his entire command were wiped out.

The great Indian chiefs started to lead their

people away from the attacking army; some went into the wilderness and carried out guerrilla warfare against the whites, while others tried to flee to Canada where they could find safety.

In 1877 Crazy Horse was killed and Sitting Bull managed to cross into Canada where he was welcomed as a hero by the Canadians. Another great Indian chief, White Bear, committed suicide in a white man's prison that same year.

Still some tribes held out and continued to attack the whites whenever the opportunity arose. But the writing was on the wall for the great tribes and in 1881 Sitting Bull surrendered and Geronimo did likewise in 1886. In 1890 Sitting Bull was killed and in 1890 the Battle of Wounded Knee was one of the last major battles in the American Indian Wars.